STEAL MY HEART

Swoon Series

J.H. CROIX

STEAL MY HEART

A road trip with some *serious* complications.

All bets are off when Mack unexpectedly crosses paths with his best friend's little sister.

Ash is off limits. Totally. They're just friends, so no problem, right? *Soooo* wrong.

Mack can't stop thinking about her.

Ash wants nothing to do with men, most certainly not grumpy Mack. Except there's one problem. He has a new ability to set her on fire.

This friends to lovers, forbidden romance is hot, intense & swoon-worthy!

Chapter One

ASH (ASHLEY)

I swung my guitar over my shoulder and stepped onto the wooden stage, casting a quick smile at the smattering of applause and whistles. "Hey y'all, I'm only here for an hour, so let's not wait."

I never waited. I launched into my first song and got lost in the music. An hour later, I walked off the stage with the cheers from the audience reverberating through me. For that hour, I'd dropped into the one place where I could forget the mess of my life.

"Great set," a voice called, just as someone else's hand slapped my ass, much harder than I preferred from anyone, much less a stranger. I cast a sharp glare over my shoulder and kept on walking. I hoped I had enough tips from filling in at the bar earlier to pad the measly paycheck I would get for playing that set.

"Ash," a voice said, slicing through the din of noise and bodies crowding around me as I tried to get to the back of the bar.

I knew that voice, but for the life of me, I couldn't place it. I did a quick scan around me. The crowd parted as a tall form became visible. The man practically swatted people out of his way as if they were nothing more than flies.

Mack Blair, all six feet and five inches of him, came into my line of sight. My body did a startling thing with my belly flipping quickly and my pulse doing a little hop, skip, and jump.

Okay, that was weird. Giving myself a mental shake, I smiled up at Mack when he stopped in front of me. "Well, hey there, Mack. What are you doing here?"

Mack's dark blue eyes swept up and down my body before searching my face. "I could ask you the same. Let's—"

I was cut off when someone bumped into me from behind, sending me colliding against Mack. Mack, with his bear-like presence, swiftly slid his arm around my back, shielding me from everyone jostling around us. "Fuck, this place is busy," he muttered.

I'd known Mack for pretty much forever. Since elementary school, at least. I was startled at the little shiver that chased over my skin at the sound of his gruff words in my ear.

"It is," I murmured in reply. "Come on, my stuff is in the back."

Mack kept his arm around my waist, basically clearing a path for us until we reached the door where I pointed. Once we pushed through the door and it swung shut behind us, his arm fell away, and I sagged against the wall.

"Wow, it went from kind of busy to a little nuts while I was playing."

I'd hugged my guitar to my chest while we walked through the crowd, so I lowered it now, holding it loosely in one hand.

Mack gave me a long look. "Good to see you, Ash."

One side of his mouth kicked up into a familiar grin, and my belly did another flip. I wondered just what in the world was going on with this reaction to Mack. I'd never responded to him like this.

"You too. I'd say let's grab a drink here, but it's pretty crowded."

"I drove past a diner down the road. Grab your stuff, and let's go get coffee or food or whatever," Mack commented.

"Sounds good. I'm actually starving," I replied as I pushed off the wall. "Follow me."

Mack and I had grown up in Stolen Hearts Valley, North Carolina, and he was one of my brother's best friends. Awareness prickled down my spine as he followed me down the hallway. I chose to ignore it, convinced my body's weird reaction to him was probably just because I was so startled to see him.

Stepping into the room where the bar owner had told me I could leave my stuff, I grabbed my purse and my bag before I looked up at him. "Jesus. I forgot how tall you were."

Mack arched a brow. "I've been this tall since my senior year in high school. Speaking of forgetting, I forgot how good you were."

"At what?" I countered as I looked at the envelope sitting on top of my purse. I ripped it open to see the check for tonight, a whopping one hundred and fifty bucks, and the cash from my tips.

"Singing and playing," Mack replied.

I held his eyes for a few beats, feeling heat on my cheeks. "Thanks," I finally managed.

I quickly counted out the tips, relieved to discover an additional one hundred bucks.

"You ready?" he asked as I stuffed the envelope in my purse.

"Yup. Let's roll."

Moments later when we stepped out into the parking lot, his gaze slid to mine as he stopped outside the door. "Do you want to follow me to the diner?"

Aaannnnd, here came the first awkward moment. "If you don't mind, I'll hitch a ride with you."

I saw the questions swirling in his eyes and held my

breath. "Of course. Come on." Mack gestured with his chin in a general direction.

Relieved he didn't ask anything else yet, I walked beside him as we crossed the parking lot to where he'd parked an all-black truck in the far corner.

Because he was Mack and a gentleman, even if a bit rough around the edges, he insisted on taking my guitar and bag from me and setting it carefully in the back. He even made sure my guitar case was properly situated so it wouldn't bounce around too much. He also insisted on getting the door for me and wouldn't even close it until I buckled my seat belt.

"I forgot how stubborn you were," I said when he climbed into the driver's seat beside me.

"Ditto. Why the hell don't you have a car, Ash?"

Oh, fuck.

I silently groaned. So much for no questions.

"Can we go to the diner first? I'd like to get some food in me before we get into all that."

"Absolutely."

It might've been a few years since I'd actually seen Mack, but I was relieved he had the same steady, easygoing manner. Not much got to Mack, and he wasn't particularly nosy either. That said, I knew I couldn't keep the truth from him.

———

"No. You're coming with me, Ash," Mack said firmly as if he expected me to simply do what he said.

Actually, there was no *as if* here. He fully expected me to do what he said. God, I just freaking *loved* getting bossed around by a man. Not.

I felt myself beginning to clench my teeth and consciously relaxed them as I glared right back at him. "You don't get to tell me what to do."

Mack took a sip of his coffee, never once breaking his

gaze from mine. He was used to people doing what he said. For one, he was usually bigger than anyone else, including most men. The other was he carried himself with this authoritative manner, and people generally did his bidding. He also had this whole rescue complex vibe and never did have enough sense to leave well enough alone.

"Mack, I'm not somebody you need to rescue. I'm fine, and I'll figure it out."

"You're not fine. You're broke, and you don't have a car. Apparently, you're planning to try to get back to Stolen Hearts Valley by hitchhiking with your freaking beloved guitar. Have you lost your goddamn mind?"

A flush raced up my neck and into my cheeks. I tried to beat back the defensiveness choking me. "I made it all the way from Colorado to Wyoming with no trouble."

"In case you haven't looked at a map lately, sugar, Wyoming is north of Colorado, so now you're farther away. Stolen Hearts is east of Colorado, not north. Does Jackson know about this grand plan?"

The moment he said my older brother's name out loud, I thought the top of my head might fly off.

Chapter Two

MACK

Ash Stone stared at me from across the table. She was pissed. Her cheeks were pink, and her blue eyes were flashing. Damn, she was gorgeous when she was mad.

"Ash, I'm not joking. It's not safe for you."

"And why's that? Because I'm a woman?" she retorted, lifting a napkin from the table and spinning it between her fingers until she twisted it into a knot. "I can take care of myself."

"Ash, please be sensible. Ride with me. Consider that your adventure if that's what you're after."

Ash's eyes looked like the sky on a stormy day just before thunder rumbled and lightning split the sky wide open. After a moment, her gaze fell from mine, and I didn't miss the way her shoulders curled inward. I'd known Ash for as long as I could remember. I knew she was tired, and worry was emanating from her in waves. I didn't know exactly what the hell happened for her to be without a car and hitch-hiking home on her own, but I wasn't leaving her here.

When her gorgeous eyes lifted again and her gaze met mine, a prickle of awareness sizzled down my spine. Okay, that was strange. If you'd asked me before how I felt about Ash, I'd have said she was like a sister. Except nothing about the way my body was reacting to her felt sisterly now. Not even a little. Her brother was one of my closest friends. Growing up, my younger sisters hung out with Ash all the time. On any given week, we were bouncing between houses, close enough that she felt like family.

When I'd looked up and seen her on that stage earlier, she'd taken my breath away as she belted out song after country song. Once the initial shock of seeing her passed, I expected my body's hyper-awareness to fade, but it wasn't fading. Not at all.

"Do you want to tell me what the hell happened, Ash?" I pressed.

She dropped the twisted napkin on the table and picked up another one to torture. "You know I was kind of seeing Kyle, right?"

"I'm not up on the gossip, Ash. I haven't been back to Stolen Hearts Valley since last Christmas. I didn't hear much other than you were traveling, playing gigs, and doing veterinarian work for the rodeo circuit. If I recall, you met some guy who brought you along to start with."

Ash nodded. "That's basically it. Anyway..." Ash licked her lips, and her lashes swept against her cheeks when she closed her eyes. Opening them again, she brushed her long brown hair off her shoulders and shrugged before her cheeks went a little pink again. "It's kind of embarrassing. It's not like I ever thought Kyle took me seriously, and I didn't want anything serious. But I got sick of him making me look like a fool. I woke up one day, and he was gone. Again. I just decided I was done with it. I sold my car about six months ago to front him a little cash. We were traveling together, so it didn't seem like a big deal. Anyway, I'm done with that, and I'm going home."

"Why didn't you call Jackson for help? You know he'd do anything for you."

"I know," she began slowly, lifting a shoulder in a small shrug, "but Jackson told me more than once that he thought Kyle was taking advantage of me. It's not like I pinned my hopes on Kyle. I didn't. After my wedding blew up with Brian, well, I was done with romance. And now I'm also done with looking like a fool."

I watched Ash for a moment as she kept fiddling with the napkin before finally dropping it and draining her coffee. At that moment, the waitress paused at our table with a pot of coffee and a bright smile. "How are you two doing?"

"I could use some more coffee," Ash replied.

"Same," I added.

The waitress filled our drinks and continued on to check on another table.

Ash lifted her head, weariness in her features. "I'll hitch a ride with you. No sense in arguing about it. The thing is, I don't have much to put toward hotels. The money I earned tonight is all I have. There's one thing, though."

"What's that?"

"Since I needed some cash, I booked some gigs to float me on the trip. It's not exactly a straight line back to Stolen Hearts."

I had *so* many questions, but I held every single one of them inside. I could see in the set of Ash's shoulders and the subtle shadows in her eyes that she was embarrassed and most definitely didn't want to explain further.

"Okay. I'm not on a tight timeframe. I was already taking care of my hotels, so that's no biggie," I said, keeping my tone light. "Where do we need to go on the way back?"

Ash stared at me for a long moment. "If we take I-90 up north and then head south after we get to Niagara Falls, that'll take me everywhere I need to go."

"That'll work. Heard that's a pretty drive."

Ash nodded, and I could practically see the wheels spinning in her brain. Finally, she said, "I'll pay you back. I just need to get back to Stolen Hearts Valley and get back to work at the vet clinic."

She and her brother were veterinarians. They'd started a clinic together on their family's old farm, which had been renovated into an outdoor adventure place for tourists looking to escape to the wilderness in comfort. In addition to that, they ran a rescue program for animals, so the vet clinic was a good fit.

Ash closed her eyes before leaning back in the booth, her brown hair a contrast to the bright red vinyl seats. Opening her eyes again, she looked over at me. "How did you end up in Wyoming?"

"Just passing through on my way home. You know I've been working with hotshot crews out in Colorado, right?"

Ash nodded. "Yeah, you stayed out West after college in Colorado. Have you been there the whole time?"

"Nah. I was there for a bit and also did a stint in Montana. Most recently, I was in Idaho. First responder work for those crews tends to be seasonal, so I followed the jobs. When Jackson let me know a position opened up in Stolen Hearts, I decided it was time to go home. How did you end up out here?" I asked, putting the focus back on her. I didn't really like thinking about why I'd stayed away from home for so long.

"You know, all this started because I was doing that vet work for the horses for that rodeo program. Remind me what an idiot I am next time you see me even thinking about dating."

I wasn't touching that comment with a ten-foot pole, so I took a long swallow of my coffee. As if conjured by my need for a distraction, so I didn't have to look too rude for ignoring Ash's comment, our waitress magically appeared with her ever-ready coffeepot to fill my almost empty cup again.

"Anything else?" she asked, her tone almost too chipper, considering it was going on midnight.

"Nah. Can you bring the bill when you get a chance?" I asked.

"Of course, hon."

"Do you already have a hotel for tonight?" I asked after the waitress departed.

Ash shook her head. "Nope. You?"

At my nod, Ash's lips twisted sideways, but she didn't say anything else.

———

Roughly a half hour later, Ash stood at the foot of the bed with her hands on her hips. "I'll take the floor," she announced.

Oh, for fuck's sake. I tossed my bag on a chair by the window before reaching up to pull the heavy drapes closed. Turning, I shook my head. "Nobody's taking the floor. It's a king-sized bed. We can keep practically three feet between us."

I was teetering on the edge of exhaustion. I'd driven for eight hours before I even ended up in this Wyoming town whose name I'd already forgotten. I was in no mood to sleep on the floor and wasn't going to put up with Ash trying to argue the point.

She met my gaze as I turned around and rolled her eyes before snorting a soft laugh. "True."

After a minor argument over who was going to shower first, I won that one and insisted Ash went first by pointing out that I had manners and Jackson would give me hell if I didn't use them.

After I'd finished showering, because I needed one to wash off a day of travel, I discovered Ash curled up in bed on the far side of the mattress, and she was already sound asleep. I'd gotten under the covers, acutely aware of her presence, but thinking it would be no big thing.

A few hours later, I came awake and rolled my head to

the side to see the clock read 4:00 a.m. I'd fallen asleep quickly despite the unexpected turn of my evening and the surprising and unsettling reaction my body was having to Ash. Until now. I'd woken in the darkness to find myself curled up behind her with her sweet bottom nestled against my achingly hard arousal.

This was awkward and inconvenient, to say the least. I had no idea who migrated toward the other first, but we were smack in the center of the bed. The scent of her curled around me. She smelled like fresh soap with a hint of her sweet musky scent underneath. I had an arm wrapped around her with my palm splayed on her belly. *Under* her T-shirt.

I silently thanked God she wasn't in just her T-shirt and underwear. Of course, the thin cotton of her leggings wasn't much of an added barrier because my cock was nestled right between the cheeks of her bottom.

I debated if it would be more likely to wake her if I moved, or if I should just pray my arousal away. It didn't help matters that she felt so fucking good, all warm and soft. She moved slightly in her sleep, shifting her bottom against me and nearly making me groan out loud.

I had a serious problem, and I needed to solve it. Fast. I decided moving was my only option. If I woke her, perhaps she wouldn't even realize we'd been curled up together.

With every cell in my body protesting, I moved away swiftly, rolling onto my back and clenching my jaw to stay silent. I held my breath, hoping and praying Ash didn't awaken. When her breathing carried on with its steady rise and fall, I finally let mine out in a slow sigh and willed my arousal to die a quick death.

Just when I thought I was out of the danger zone, Ash rolled over, curling up against me and hooking her knee over one of my thighs.

Dear God. What sin had I committed to be forced through this penance?

My eyes fluttered open, and sensation filtered into my awareness. The rhythmic rise and fall of Mack's chest under my palm. The warmth of his thigh where my knee was hooked over it. Mack was warm all over, and I didn't want to move. His arm was wrapped around my back and his palm rested at the base of my spine, his fingers teasing the waistband of my leggings.

As soon as I absorbed the reality of my situation, I slammed my eyes shut as my heartbeat kicked off at a rapid pace. Considering that I was plastered against his side, I knew if he was awake, he could probably feel every thud of my heart against his ribs.

I could feel my cheeks heat in the darkness and prayed like crazy that he wasn't awake yet. Cautiously opening my eyes again, I glanced at his face. His profile was in shadow, but his eyes were blessedly closed.

Just beyond his shoulder, I could see the glowing numbers of the clock on the nightstand. It was 5:00 a.m. Taking stock, I realized we were mostly over toward his side of the bed, which meant I was the one with the wandering body and hands. I was mortified beyond belief. I was curled against him so tightly that I didn't know if I could detach without him noticing. As if it weren't bad enough already, I could feel the slick heat between my thighs. Apparently, I was capable of getting insanely aroused in my sleep. Who knew? Certainly not me.

I started to move in increments, and my knee barely brushed against the evidence of his arousal. Oh. My. God. Heat suffused my entire body, and I felt my core clench in response. No matter what my mind thought, my body was having an entirely different conversation with Mack.

I tried to keep my breathing quiet, but that only seemed to send my pulse into the stratosphere. I needed away from him and prayed he didn't wake up. I rolled away swiftly, just far enough that we weren't touching anymore. I worried too much motion and crawling all the way across the bed would wake him. He might not know I'd been plastered to him like a desperate hussy, but I'd noticed his arousal. I figured only one of us needed to be embarrassed.

I tried to go back to sleep, but my body wasn't having it. I couldn't shut off the need pulsing through me. Even worse, I kept imagining the feel of his hard, muscled body over mine, causing me to shift my legs restlessly in order to relieve the ache there.

Chapter Four

MACK

It was only five thirty a.m., but I hoped Ash had fallen back asleep after she threw herself away from me. I couldn't wait any longer, so I slipped out of bed to shower. I didn't even bother with a cold one and literally took matters into my own hands, picturing Ash until my release spurted against the wall in the shower.

Not much later when I came out of the bathroom, I found Ash leaning against the headboard with the bedside table lamp on. Her breath was coming in sharp pants, and her skin was flushed. I knew without a doubt what she'd been doing. And I was so fucked.

———

"Back off," I warned.

The guy who just groped Ash's ass as she walked by after coming off the stage gave me a drunken glare. "Who the fuck are you?" he slurred.

I shouldered him out of the way without bothering to answer his question.

Ash startled me when she replied, "He's my boyfriend. Now, back off."

Okay, whatever. I walked next to Ash, keeping her close with an arm around her shoulders until we pushed through a door into the hallway.

Ash looked up at me, blowing a loose lock of hair out of her eyes when she leaned against the wall in the narrow hallway. "Thanks."

"Boyfriend?" I asked.

"Easiest answer," she replied with a light shrug although her cheeks tinged pink. "I probably shouldn't—"

Her words stopped abruptly when I shook my head. "I don't care. You want me to play your boyfriend for the rest of the shows you have booked? It's probably the easiest way to keep the assholes off your back."

Ash pressed a palm flat against the wall and pushed away as she dipped her chin in acknowledgment. I followed her into yet another small room crowded with odds and ends. She gathered her things while I put her beloved guitar in its case. After she checked with the bar owner and tucked her paycheck away, we stepped out into the night.

It was summer in Montana, and the sky spread like black velvet above us with stars sprinkled like glitter across the surface, a distant sparkle in the darkness.

Ash stopped, leaning her head back to look up. "It's beautiful here," she said softly. With the muted sounds of the bar behind us, her voice was clear in the crisp summer air.

"It is." My eyes scanned the sky, lingering on the moon hanging in a crescent over the mountain ranges surrounding us.

Moments later, we were inside my truck, and I glanced over at Ash. "How many more gigs do you have booked?"

Ash angled her head to the side. "Eight. Is that gonna be a problem?"

"Absolutely not. Just helps to know." The engine rumbled to life when I pressed the start button.

When I'd pointed out I thought her original plan to hitchhike home with the money she earned from gigs was insane—because it was—Ash had gotten defensive. I'd left it alone since then because now she was riding with me. Her not-so-sensible plan wasn't happening, so there was no point in arguing about it.

The information had come in fits and starts over the past few days, but I'd pieced together her life for the past couple of years. In short, some guy she had something like a friends-with-benefits relationship with had persuaded her it would be fun to travel as a veterinarian on the rodeo circuit. She worked sporadically while he rode the circuit and left her high and dry periodically. Apparently, he left her behind in a hotel in Colorado for another fling a few weeks before our paths collided in Wyoming.

I still wasn't sure why the hell she'd left Stolen Hearts to begin with, but I wasn't one to judge. Lots of people, myself included, made choices that didn't always make sense for reasons no one else understood.

"Did you have a specific date you needed to be back in Stolen Hearts?" Ash asked as I drove toward the hotel. I'd stopped and reserved a room earlier this evening after dropping her off at the bar to get ready for her gig.

"I finished my last job in Idaho and decided it was time to head home. They've got an opening on the first responder crew in Stolen Hearts Valley. I'm sure Jackson mentioned that," I commented, referring to the fact her brother worked on the same first responder crew I'd be joining.

"How come you stayed away so long?" Ash asked.

I didn't mind her question. She knew my life just as I knew hers. She was running from something. Meanwhile, I had my own ghosts and needed a change of pace. It was hard for years after my younger sister Krista died. Getting away from the memories helped for a while, but I was finally starting to realize that maybe I just needed to face them.

I could feel Ash's eyes on me, but I resisted the urge to look. I knew I needed to come to terms with what happened to Krista, but it still sucked, and it still hurt.

"I bet you still miss her. I know I do," Ash said softly, somehow reading my thoughts.

Ash was usually guarded emotionally. So for her to say that aloud, I knew she meant it deeply.

"Of course I miss her. But I'm ready to go home. Jackson said it's fine whenever I get there, so there's no timetable."

"Of course he did," Ash said with a small sigh. "You're escorting me home."

I slid my eyes sideways to see her wrinkling her nose. "Maybe so, but it's just because he loves you, Ash."

"I know. Thank you again."

"No need to thank me."

"It wasn't a good plan for me to try to hitchhike. It's not safe, and I pride myself on not doing stupid things."

"Well, your friend there didn't leave you in the best situation as far as money and transportation."

Ash's laugh was bitter. "No, he didn't. It's all good, though. I needed to shake him loose."

Hours later, I lay in bed, staring at the dark ceiling. Unfortunately, sleep was hard to come by. I was confident I wouldn't get a good night's sleep until I wasn't trapped in hotel rooms with Ash night after night.

After the first night, I made sure to get rooms with two beds. We had an argument about getting two separate rooms, but I knew Ash was short on cash. She was too proud and stubborn to let me foot the bill for an extra room, so I was stuck with being tortured.

I'd gotten accustomed to the sound of her breathing. Rolling my head to the side, I saw the outline of her shoulder and the rise of her breasts with every breath from the parking lot lights that filtered through the curtains. I didn't need to notice that she'd shoved the covers down around her waist and her tank top was showing a strip of skin across her belly.

Fuck me. I forcibly rolled over and stared at the wall. Although we were tiptoeing around each other, there was no mistaking the electricity between us once we were alone. We distracted ourselves with stupid television shows and takeout at night, but even hotel rooms with two beds felt crowded with the sparks bouncing around in the air.

I was wrestling with my desire for Ash. She was Jackson's little sister, and I couldn't forget that. I imagined Jackson wouldn't appreciate me giving her a ride if he knew my cock was hard every night when I was alone with her.

The next morning, I woke after a shitty night's sleep and got in the shower first. Once again, I took care of business. The only way to stay halfway sane with Ash was to jack off every morning in the shower. I was toweling dry when the door opened, and Ash squeaked.

I was frozen for a beat when my eyes landed on her. She was wearing a tank top and a fitted pair of shorts. Unfortunately, on Ash, everything turned me on. Her taut nipples pressed against the thin fabric. I belatedly realized I was completely naked as I stood in the shower with a towel frozen on my head where I'd been rubbing it through my hair.

Chapter Five

ASH

My eyes roamed over Mack's body, greedily soaking in every inch of him. It's not as if I didn't know Mack was built. But Mack naked with his skin damp from the shower was something else. Every inch of him was honed. Mack was a big man with broad shoulders, and heavy arms and thighs. Yet somehow, the lines of his body were sleek. He had a smattering of dark hair on his chest, and a tempting trail of hair led straight to the promised land.

My naughty eyes disobeyed me entirely when I tried and failed to keep from looking there. Oh. My. God. The V of muscles tapered down like an off-ramp on the highway showing me where to go. Even his cock was gorgeous—thick and heavy against his thigh.

My nipples were so hard they ached. When my eyes made their way back up to Mack's face, I knew my cheeks were bright red. I snapped my mouth shut and spun away just as he whipped his towel around his waist.

"Sorry," I squeaked as I scurried out of the doorway and slammed the door shut behind me.

I was only half awake when I rolled out of bed to hurry to the bathroom, which was why I hadn't even noticed Mack wasn't in bed. I was *wide*-awake now. I yanked on a pair of sweatpants and sat at the foot of my bed, trying to calm my racing pulse and get some desperately needed air into my lungs.

I felt like I was losing my mind. After almost two years of being close to numb when it came to men, it confused the hell out of me that my body was practically on fire for Mack. I'd known Mack for so long. I could remember his mother yelling at him and Jackson when they got in trouble for putting frogs in Evie's bed when I was spending the night there.

Not once during all the years I'd known him had I ever experienced even a flicker of attraction toward Mack. Now, it just wouldn't quit.

I heard the bathroom doorknob turning and took a deep breath, instantly aware that I forgot to throw something on over my tank top. The moment my body knew Mack was about to come through the door, my nipples thought they needed to personally greet him. Oh, God.

Just play it cool. You can totally do this.

That fervent hope went up in smoke the moment Mack stepped out of the bathroom. Fuck my life. He wasn't wearing a shirt. Again. He had on the sweatpants he tended to wear when he was relaxing. They rested low on his hips, just low enough to make my mouth water. Up until a few minutes ago, I only had my imagination to go on as for his delicious V muscles and where that teasing trail of dark hair led.

I knew before, hypothetically, but now I *knew*. If you know what I mean.

I pasted a polite smile on my face. "Sorry about that. I wasn't really awake and didn't notice you weren't in bed," I said, pointlessly waving my hand in the air in no particular direction

The moment Mack's ridiculously sexy chest came into my line of sight, my eyes were like freaking magnets and clamped onto him. Ugh. In the soft light cast from the lamp I'd turned on, my eyes traveled over his gleaming skin, following down to that V and that trail of dark hair. Oh God. I needed to stop thinking about Mack naked.

My mouth watered, and I had to squeeze my thighs together. I wanted to lick him all over. He was super lickable.

I leaped up from the bed. "Mind if I shower?" I blurted out.

Still holding a towel in his hand, Mack lifted it and scrubbed it over his damp hair. That only made matters worse. Mack with his dark brown hair mussed and damp was so sexy that my belly was doing somersaults. It felt as if sparks were raining from the sky over my body, setting my nerves alight until I was tingling all over.

"Course not," he drawled, gesturing toward the bathroom.

Apparently, he had the capacity for his conversation and coordinated hand motions to actually make sense, instead of the flailing I seemed to do whenever I was nervous around him.

I raced to my suitcase where it sat on a chair in the corner and blindly grabbed a pair of jeans and a T-shirt, remembering at the last second that I would need under-wear and a bra. I *really* needed a bra. I needed to smash my nipples into submission, or at least add enough fabric between them and the sight of Mack that it wasn't obvious my nipples were waving at him.

———

"You want to what?"

"Stop for a day or so in the Badlands," Mack explained.

I opened my mouth to say no but caught myself before I acted like an ungrateful bitch. "I'd love to see the Badlands."

That was actually true. It was just that every stop we made only extended the torture of trying to get my body under control. My body was behaving like an oppositional teenager and was in all-out rebellion against my rational, sane mind.

I felt Mack's eyes slide to me, and I looked over. "Sure, let's stop," I added for good measure.

"I figure since we can't do a direct route anyway, there's no sense in trying to rush it. You have two days before that gig in Michigan. After Michigan, I figure we can decide when to angle south. Be a pretty drive. You know, we'll be less than a day's drive from Niagara Falls. Ever been?"

He turned his eyes back to the highway in front of us. Interstate 90 was taking us through the upper part of the United States. Of course, my eyes, ever willful, lingered on the flex of his forearm as he rolled the steering wheel under his hand when the highway took a subtle curve. That was how bad I had it. Mack's hands turned me on. But it wasn't just his hands. It was his forearms, his shoulders, his jaw, his nose, and every freaking inch of his body. And I was so screwed because I'd actually seen just about every inch of his body.

A part of me wrestled with whether this attraction—or rather, raw burning lust—was a one-way street, yet my body sure didn't think so. I hadn't missed the flares of heat that went up in his dark blue eyes whenever they snagged with mine. I thought he had things more under control than me, though. I had it so bad for Mack that for the past three nights in a row I'd masturbated in the bathroom in the middle of the night in an effort to fall sleep.

We hadn't laid a single hand on each other, and I'd had more orgasms in the week I'd been traveling with him than I'd had with any man. Ever.

"The Badlands, here we come," I said, trying to steel myself to tolerate the madness of the heat pulsing through my veins. It was bad enough we were sharing a room every night, but during the day, I was trapped in the truck with him. The space felt so small.

Chapter Six

ASH

"Hey, baby," a man's voice said over my shoulder right before his palm grabbed my ass and squeezed hard enough to make me jump.

I spun around. "I'm not your baby, and keep your hands to yourself."

"Oh, come on, baby," the guy muttered.

I opened my mouth to spew a retort, but the guy was suddenly lifted off his feet. Mack came into view when he set the guy down a few feet away as if he were a toy. "She said to keep your hands to yourself."

I wasn't usually the kind of girl who got all wound up by seeing a man be protective. Apparently, I *was* that kind a girl when it came to Mack. A thrill chased down my spine and goose bumps prickled over my skin as Mack stepped in front of me, all tall, growly, and so freaking manly and sexy.

"Let's get a booth," Mack murmured as he leaned down to be heard over the noise.

The feel of his lips brushing against my ear sent heat chasing through me, and I almost moaned out loud. After I wrestled my rebellious body under control—hell, it was like yanking on the reins of a galloping wild pony—I replied, "Sounds like a plan."

I couldn't help it. Whenever Mack led me through a crowd, my body spun like a little top. His big palm landed on the side of my waist as he guided me through the room. By virtue of his size, the crowd usually parted for him.

In another moment, Mack magically found us a booth in the far corner after a heavy wink at one of the waitresses while she was cleaning it. I leaned back in the wooden bench seat and let out a sigh.

"You okay, Ash?" Mack drawled as he snagged a menu from where it was tucked between the salt and pepper shakers in the middle of the table.

I wasn't about to tell him that I was sighing in relief at having a few feet between us. I was in serious danger of making a move on Mack, and I knew it was a *really* bad idea.

Mack would probably have far more sense than me and point out just how *bad* of an idea it was, leaving me to deal with that awkward rejection for days. Maybe even weeks or months. Because it wasn't as though he was going anywhere in my life. We might not be cramped together day and night after this trip, but our lives were still inextricably entwined in Stolen Hearts Valley.

Even worse, maybe he wouldn't turn me away, and we'd end up having bad sex. Because I was really good at finding guys who sucked in bed and then staying with them.

There was a third option, though. Mack wouldn't turn me away, the sex would be as good as my body thought it would be, and then all hell would break loose. Because that would make it even more awkward. I wasn't looking for love. Hell, I gave up on love after my fiancé, who I thought I loved even though he sucked in bed, was getting ready for our wedding the very same morning his girlfriend sent me screenshots of their graphic texts, dick pics and all.

I'd sworn off men as far as looking for romance, then like a fool, I decided a friends-with-benefits thing would be right up my alley. Kyle had been hot, cute, and totally flirtatious, so my body thought he'd be great in bed too. I no longer trusted my body's radar when it came to guesstimating the potential for a man in the sack.

Unfortunately, I hadn't understood something about myself before I started that mess. I wasn't really cut out for the whole friends-with-benefits situation. That wasn't to say I fantasized about a picket fence and two-point-five kids with Kyle. No, I definitely did not. I just wasn't the kind of person to be so casual even when I didn't really want something serious. Kyle was *all* about casual. The dynamics of our arrangement dented my ego more than I wished I'd allowed.

If the sex with Mack was good, then I'd be in real trouble.

Mack's not an asshole, my treacherous mind whispered.

No, but a good vibrator or even my fingers will do the trick for the rest of my life, my smart mind countered quickly.

Yeah, but what about kids?

Fuck you, I told that stupid part of my brain. I *had* always wanted kids, but I could adopt or do the sperm donation thing. I didn't have to be traditional.

Mack would be a good father. You know him.

Oh, shut the fuck up.

These were the crazy directions my brain went when I let myself think too long about how much I wanted Mack.

"Ash?" Mack prompted as he looked up from the menu in his hands.

"Oh, sorry. I zoned out," I belatedly replied. I wasn't about to tell Mack I was thinking about him and having a baby. Jesus, I had gone seriously crazy. I chalked it up to the lust addling my brain. "I'm just tired. Anything good?"

Talking about the food options at this bar off the interstate in South Dakota seemed like an excellent distraction. Unfortunately—I said that a lot when it came to Mack—my eyes got caught on his hands. Although he was a big man, his hands were elegant yet rugged at the same time. He had long, nimble fingers. I could just imagine the magic they might wring from my body.

"They probably have good burgers," he said. "It's crowded, and I noticed plenty of local license plates in the parking lot. That's always a good sign. Plus, they've got spicy fries. Your favorite."

He looked over with a wink and a slow, teasing grin. My nipples did their little salute thing, and I thanked God I wore a sweatshirt on this chilly summer night.

"Awesome," I managed even though my voice came out raspy. Once again, I became aware of my slick, swollen pussy. Have I mentioned we hadn't laid a finger on each other yet? The state of my body was something to behold. I felt like I was constantly primed.

I'd read about people who got off on edging each other for days. I never really thought much about any of it, but now I understood. I didn't really want to do it, but I understood the insanely arousing effect it could have. If—a big, *real* big if—anything happened between Mack and me, and it was good, I was pretty sure I was going to go off like I'd never gone off in my entire life.

The following day—after another night in a hotel room that felt as small as a closet despite the existence of two beds and more than enough space for two people to tolerate each other—Mack and I set off on a hike in the famed Badlands.

Mack, being the planner he was, had looked up a trail and wanted to beat the crowds, so we were up at sunrise. As the sun crested the horizon, it cast a rosy pink glow on a rock face ahead while we walked.

"It is beautiful here," I commented when we stopped along the trail to look out over a valley. "I understand the name now."

Mack's eyes slid to mine. "What name?"

"The Badlands. It's gorgeous, but it's tough looking." The steep canyons and rock formations with layered colors were stunning.

Mack nodded. "So true. Come on."

As I hurried along behind him, I couldn't resist adding, "You set a hell of a pace."

Mack stopped, his grin teasing as he waited for me to catch up. "Did you get out of shape?"

"I think our standards for being in shape are different," I replied as I stopped beside him and rested a hand on my hip. "You rescue people for a living. I don't."

Mack chuckled, and I willed my body not to react to that. Of course, my will was nothing compared to my bossy nerves. It didn't seem to matter what Mack did because I always had some kind of reaction. Just now, a prickle of heat chased over my skin, and butterflies tickled my belly. Staring into his eyes was dangerous for my sanity, so I averted my gaze.

"How much farther are we going?" I asked, finally looking back toward him when I thought I had my pulse under control.

"We can turn back if you want."

"No way. I'm not gonna cop out. Come on."

I strode past Mack, who turned and easily caught up to me with his long stride. Glancing to my side, I commented, "No fair. Your legs are longer than mine. Every step you take probably counts for an extra six inches. I should get extra credit."

Mack grinned and winked. "You always did like to be an A-plus student."

I rolled my eyes, and we kept hiking. After we made it to the predetermined high-point on the hike, I was relieved to discover the elevation went down on the opposite side of this loop trail. Despite my unsettled reactions to Mack, I was glad we knew each other well enough that our silence was comfortable.

While I wasn't thrilled with the way my body went haywire around him, I was relieved to be traveling with him. It was a much better option than trying to bum rides from strangers and hoping for the best. Jackson had made it abundantly clear he was glad Mack happened to find me.

I kept telling myself I was going to get over my response to Mack. It worried me because I'd sworn off men and thought it would be easy. If I could react like this to an old friend, that meant it was possible with someone else. I didn't trust my judgment when it came to men.

My mind spun back to the morning of my disastrous wedding that never happened. I'd had the pleasure of looking at sexy photographs of my fiancé with a woman who was gracious enough to tell me she thought it was only fair I should know he'd been in a "committed" relationship with her for six months before she learned he was engaged. Maybe gracious wasn't the best way to describe it, but I did appreciate her honesty.

I mentally shoved those thoughts away. No need to dwell on how stupid I felt. It was one thing to have someone cheat on you, but it was another to realize they intended to carry on with it after the wedding. Of course, the humiliation of it was all made worse by the fact I had to cancel a giant wedding. Ugh. It was awful. I wasn't even a little interested in trying to be serious with anyone after that.

Enter Kyle—sexy rodeo rider, consummate flirt, and charming enough to persuade me that a little casual fun was worth it. Sadly, my ego had been bruised enough that I tried to play along with Kyle's way of life for over a year even though I found it pointless. He was on the boring side in bed, probably because his ego was much bigger than his skill set.

My shredded pride finally had enough, and I was ready to return to Stolen Hearts Valley and ignore the sympathetic glances from friends and family. I thought it would be easy to carve men out of my life because my capacity for desire seemed to have died.

I was tired of thinking about any of this and annoyed that my weird, out-of-the-blue reaction to Mack was dredging it all up again. A sharp cry instantly pulled me out of that loop of recrimination.

I heard another voice just as Mack glanced over his shoulder. "I'm going to run ahead and see what's going on."

"Right behind you," I said as I broke into a jog.

Moments later, we were standing beside a couple on the trail, and the woman was clutching her very pregnant belly. Her husband, who looked fit and tough, was basically useless. His eyes bounced from his wife, to Mack, and then to me. "I think she's gone into labor."

"How far along is she?" Mack asked, his tone all no-nonsense.

"Eight months and three weeks."

Mack cast a look at them. "And you decided to go hiking today?"

"It's just a hike," the woman protested before she emitted another sharp cry while her face contorted in pain.

Mack glanced at me. "Call 911."

I had emergency services on the line in a matter of seconds. Once I explained the situation, they asked if it was possible for the woman in labor to walk to the base of the trail. Glancing over to see her on the ground with her face twisted in pain, I answered without asking. "That's doubtful. It looks like she's going to have the baby right here."

"We'll be there in about twenty minutes, ma'am."

Considering it had taken Mack and me almost thirty minutes to get to this point on the hike, I figured they'd be hauling ass. After I hung up, I glanced at Mack. "Is there anything I can do?"

"What do you have in your backpack? We could use a jacket, or shirt, or something to put under her hips. If you have any water, that would be great."

"I have both," I said, quickly shrugging my backpack off my shoulders.

Meanwhile, the husband still wasn't particularly helpful. He kept pacing in a circle and then kneeling to see how his wife was doing before putting his hands over his face and running them through his hair repeatedly.

Thank God for Mack. His steady and calm presence made the situation less stressful. Although I wasn't the one in pain, I was concerned about the baby being born out here. I knew women had been giving birth for millennia in a variety of difficult locations, so I hoped for the best and prayed there were no complications.

The twenty minutes ticked by fast and slow. The baby seemed to be on a speeding highway. At one point, Mack coached the woman. "You're gonna need to push. Now," he said.

"I'm scared!" the woman screamed in reply.

"Your baby's not. The baby is coming whether you like it or not. I can see the head, and we need you to push," Mack replied, his tone calm and level.

Her body seemed to take over. Only minutes later, Mack was holding the baby as he asked me to pull a medical kit out of his backpack. Without even breaking a sweat, he snipped the umbilical cord and handed the baby to the mother. The baby was breathing in angry cries.

The emergency team literally showed up a minute after that. Mack left them to stabilize the mother and baby for transport. Once Mack gave his phone number to the husband who'd finally calmed down so he could call later and give us an update, we resumed our hike down the trail.

Mack rinsed off in a nearby stream. After we had walked in silence for several minutes, I glanced over at him. "Have you ever delivered a baby before?"

Mack let out a surprised laugh. "Hell no. They train us on it, but honestly, I prayed I wouldn't ever need to deal with it."

"Well, you were totally calm."

"Good thing I can fake it," he added with another laugh.

When his eyes met mine, for the first time ever, I saw a

flicker of vulnerability in his gaze. "Wow, you can actually get scared," I commented.

"Oh, yeah. I just deal with it at the moment and then get the shakes later if it's really bad. I gotta say, that was definitely not easy. I was worried there might be a complication."

My breath left my chest in a rush as emotion crashed through me. There was something so comforting about Mack's constant sense of calm, yet knowing that it wasn't that easy for him struck me hard.

At that moment, as Mack and I stared at each other, it felt as if electricity sparked between us, sizzling through my body in a fiery jolt. Unsettled, I looked away and began walking again.

Hours later, we stood at the hotel desk while Mack politely argued with the receptionist. "Sir, I'm so sorry, but we don't have a double room available."

"Do you have two rooms?" Mack countered.

"No, sir. It's early though. Sometimes people cancel, so you can check later if you'd like."

Without thinking, I shifted on my feet, and my hand brushed against Mack. Small problem. That subtle touch, which had no erotic intention whatsoever, sent sensation spinning through my body. It felt as if I was constantly on edge around him, and any incidental contact only served to stoke the fire.

"Don't worry about it. It's just one night," I offered.

Mack's eyes held mine, his gaze searching. After a moment, he shrugged and turned back to the receptionist. "Okay. That'll be fine."

Chapter Seven

MACK

Fine, my ass. Sharing a bed with Ash was anything but *fine*. I was in for a sleepless night, and I just prayed that I didn't actually fall asleep and end up twined around her again.

In an effort to make sure we didn't have much time alone in the room, I suggested we go out for drinks at a bar after dinner. It turned out, the bar was having an open mic night. That was all fine and good until Ash decided to go up and play. Ash's voice was divine—throaty and raspy with a Southern twang that strummed every cord in my body. Watching her was transporting.

By the time her voice rang out the last note, every hair on my body was standing. I took a gulp of my ice-cold beer and willed myself to get a grip. As I had learned was the case whenever Ash performed, plenty of men crowded near when she walked off stage, trying to get into her pants for the night.

I tried to tell myself she was an old friend and I would do it for any woman, but once again, I stood and threaded through the crowd to her side. I could tell myself that was my motivation except for the jolt of possessiveness that struck me every time somebody laid a hand on her.

Tonight, because she wasn't formally performing, she handed over the guitar she'd borrowed. We lost the table where we'd been sitting, but we found another toward the back. Ash's cheeks were flushed, and her eyes glimmering with vitality. She thrived on playing.

"Can I have a sip of your beer?" she asked.

I chuckled. "Left mine at the table when I came to walk you over. I'll stick with water now since I'm driving."

A waitress stopped by at that moment. "Beer for you?" I asked, looking at Ash for confirmation.

"Actually, I'll take some water and a whiskey on the rocks."

After we ordered, the waitress hurried off, promising us our drinks quickly.

"Whiskey?" I queried with a lift of my brow.

Ash leaned back in her chair and smoothed a palm over her hair. "I like whiskey. I was gonna steal a sip of your beer 'cause I thought you had it. The water will kill my thirst, and then I can enjoy some whiskey." She canted her head to the side, regarding me quietly before adding, "You don't have to come to my rescue and escort me every time I get off stage."

I shrugged. "I'd do it for any woman."

"Is this some sort of I'm-your-friend's-little-sister thing?"

I shook my head. Because it wasn't, but then it was. "You know damn well if Jackson happened to be around, and Evie was walking through a crowd, and guys were grabbing her ass that he'd be over there in a hot second."

Ash laughed softly. "Good point."

The evening passed easily. Knowing Ash as long as I had, there was no shortage of topics to discuss. With each of us having taken our own detours away from Stolen Hearts Valley, we had plenty to catch up on.

For the most part, I managed to keep distracted after establishing a few silent ground rules for myself.

Don't let my eyes drop below Ash's. Don't linger on the way her bottom lip was so plump and tempting. And for fuck's sake, don't stare into her eyes for too long.

Whenever that happened, it felt as if a charge began to fill the air between us. I didn't know if Ash was wrestling as powerfully as I was with this startling, unexpected raw and fierce desire, but I knew something was there. I saw it in her eyes whenever we looked at each other for too long.

"What do you mean you didn't know what happened?" she asked. She was in the middle of explaining what happened when she called off her wedding roughly two years ago.

I shrugged. "Ash, all I knew was you canceled your wedding. I was in Montana about to get on a plane before the sun came up. As it was, I was only landing an hour before the ceremony. Jackson texted me and told me I could cancel my flight unless I wanted to visit anyway. I did want to visit anyway, but the timing wasn't great. The money in Montana was good since I was getting a ton of overtime that summer."

Ash finished off her second glass of whiskey. She was tipsy, more so than I'd ever seen her on this trip. She let out a deep sigh, her cheeks going pink as she rolled her eyes. "Oh, God. Well, I guess you might as well hear it from me."

Just then, our waitress passed by again, picking up Ash's empty glass and my empty glass of water.

"Another round?"

"I'll stick with water," I replied.

"He's driving, so that's exactly why I'll take another," Ash said with a lopsided smile.

After our waitress disappeared, I looked at Ash. "Okay, lay it on me. Now you've got me curious."

Admittedly, I was far more curious about why Ash called off her wedding now than I'd ever been before. Because before I hadn't been so attracted to her that she left me on fire most nights.

Ash traced her fingertip along the grain of the wood on the table before lifting her eyes to mine again. "It's stupid and embarrassing."

"You don't have to tell me," I added quickly. Because she didn't. I didn't know why I really cared in the first place.

Ash's teeth dented her bottom lip as she regarded me. I could practically see the gears grinding in her thoughts. I sincerely doubted she knew the effect biting her lip had on me. Because all I could think about was what her lips might feel like underneath mine.

Fucking focus, I said to myself.

It felt as if Ash had grabbed the steering wheel in my mind, and it was driving my thoughts in all kinds of crazy directions.

For years, I'd been driven to stay on the move and leave the pain of one horrible, tragic moment that I couldn't ever repair in the dust. I'd long ago accepted that my internal restlessness and penance added up to never being serious with any woman. It involved too much, a vulnerability I didn't even want to touch. I preferred to keep it hidden behind sarcasm.

I wasn't even sure why I'd finally decided to return to Stolen Hearts Valley. If it weren't for encountering Ash, there was a high likelihood I might've already changed my mind.

Ash lifted a shoulder in a small shrug, her cheeks cresting with a hint of pink when she finally released her bottom lip. "I might as well tell you. You'll find out soon enough once we get back home."

Cocking my head to the side, I mirrored her shrug. "Maybe it's not as bad as you think."

Her brows hitched up, and her mouth twisted in a bitter smile. "On the morning of the wedding, Brian's other girl-friend," she began with air quotes around other girlfriend, "sent me texts. Plenty of them. Dick pics, them together, and so on. Apparently, she'd just found out he was engaged, and he'd been seeing her for months. She said they were in a committed relationship."

"What the fuck?" I experienced a flash of anger on Ash's behalf. "Brian is a fucking idiot. I'm sorry he cheated on you, but wouldn't you rather know before the wedding?"

"Oh, sure. It would've sucked to find out after the wedding. But that wasn't the worst part. Along with the dick pics I got to see, she sent screenshots of comments he made about me in a text to most of our friends." Ash leaned her head back in the booth and let out a groan. "It was awful. She even helpfully included a text I'd sent to Brian. Fortunately, it didn't include my face, but it did include my boobs. I'm guessing she got her hands on his phone."

"Wow. She was really going for the bitch award."

Ash shrugged. "Maybe. At least she told me before the wedding. So yeah, it really sucked. I'm relieved I found out in the long run, but it was awful, and it was totally embarrassing."

"Sounds like Brian found himself exactly who he deserved," I commented, my anger rumbling under the surface. "Should I kick his ass when we get back home?" I was dead serious.

Ash's eyes widened before she let out a startled laugh. "No need. It's been two years. I don't even think he lives in Stolen Hearts Valley anymore. Jackson offered to do the same—"

I cut in. "Of course he did. Brian deserved it."

Ash rolled her eyes. "Maybe so, but I didn't want any more drama than we'd already had. Trust me, it sucks to have everybody see your boobs, and canceling a wedding is a big deal. The logistics are a nightmare, and I still had a ton of stuff to pay off. Long story short, I swore off ever taking romance seriously," Ash added with a determined lilt to her tone.

"For good?"

Why the hell are you asking that? I cast a mental glare at that snide questioning voice in my head.

I did *not* want to contemplate why I was wondering if I had a shot with Ash.

Ash held my gaze and nodded. "For good. It's not worth it."

"What about the last guy you were seeing? Kyle, right?"

Ash snorted and rolled her eyes. "Kyle. That was just stupid. We weren't serious, and I guess I got sick of him playing the field all the time. He wasn't cheating because we were never exclusive, but it just got old."

I didn't know why, but the questions just kept marching out of my mouth. "Well, if you weren't serious—"

My stupid mouth got a clue when Ash sent me a hard glare. "No, we weren't serious, but I got tired of being the friend with benefits while he fucked around with plenty of other people."

"Got it."

As though the waitress knew I'd almost gotten myself in trouble, she moved to our table after serving drinks at a table behind us and very conveniently interrupted our conversation. "Can I get you two anything else?"

Ash shook her head. "I'm all set. You?"

"I'm good."

"I'll get your check. Where are y'all staying?"

"The place right down the street," I replied.

"Nice place. They're usually full."

The moment she said that, I recalled we were stuck in a room with one bed. Fuck.

Chapter Eight

MACK

An hour later, I stared at the single queen-size bed in the hotel room and silently cursed. I'd tried to convince myself I could handle this.

"I'll go check at the desk again, maybe someone cancelled a reservation," I muttered.

We were in a touristy area, so I knew my luck probably wasn't going to hold, but I'd be damned if I wasn't going to try. Ash was silent as we rode the elevator back down to the reception area. Her long legs kept up with me as I strode quickly over to the desk.

The man checking people in was busy, but two families later, he glanced up. "Is everything okay with your room?" he asked with a quick look back and forth between us.

"It's fine, but we reserved a double room. When we checked in earlier, the guy here said to check back in case anyone cancelled."

The man's expression stayed smooth and bland. "Okay, let me see what we have."

He went through the motions of checking his computer screen, but I was pretty sure he knew the answer before he finally gave in. His eyes met mine with a polite smile. "I'm so sorry, sir, but the hotel is still full, and we haven't had any cancellations."

"Are you sure?" Ash chimed in at my shoulder.

"Definitely. I'm very sorry. I would offer to see if I can find another hotel nearby, but—"

I cut him off. "I know, you're the only place nearby. We'll make do."

I didn't wait for anything further from him and stalked back to the elevators with Ash hurrying to catch up to me.

"I'm sure it'll be fine," she said once we were in the elevator.

I punched the number for our floor before looking at her. "Sure."

She leaned against the wall across from me. Maybe six feet separated us. It was no matter. We were alone in a small space. Fiery sparks began to fill the space, bouncing off each other with the air around us nearly snapping and crackling with electricity.

This chemistry that wouldn't fucking quit between Ash and me was irritating the hell out of me. I thought it was a fluke at first since I hadn't seen her in years. This stupid trip felt like it was taking forever because she had shows scheduled. I was seriously considering buying her a plane ticket and sending her home.

Before I realized my thoughts had turned themselves into words, I was speaking. "Whaddya say I just buy you a plane ticket?"

Ash had been looking at the floor. Her head snapped up, her eyes locking to mine. "What?"

"I'll buy you a plane ticket."

"Where?"

"Home."

Her mouth dropped open, and then she gave her head a quick shake before snapping it shut. "I have more gigs booked. I might not be famous, but it's all I have for money right now. I'm not gonna flake just because you're in a hurry to get home. How about you take a plane, and I'll take your truck? Or better yet, I'll hitchhike the rest of the way like I planned. I don't need your help." Her eyes were flashing, and her cheeks were pink as she lifted her chin and glared at me.

"Why are you so pissed?"

"Because...you just—" Her words broke off as she let out a growl of frustration. "I didn't ask you to give me a ride. But here we are. I know you told Jackson all about it, so I can't just do my own thing without hearing about it from him. I realize that you're going out of your way." She paused, lowering her tone after she took a deep, shuddering breath. "I appreciate everything you've done, Mack, but let's just forget it. I'll find my own way tomorrow."

"Look, it's no big deal," I heard myself saying, suddenly feeling like an ass. "It's just—" I cut that sentence off. Real quick.

I didn't know how the hell to explain to her what the problem was. I wanted her like nobody's business, but she was Jackson's little sister, and she'd just told me romance was off the table for her. Although I knew chemistry when I felt it, and I knew it wasn't a one-way street between us, it still didn't feel right to act on it.

Ash and I were a bad idea... a *really* bad idea.

"What? What's the problem? You're the one who said—" Just as Ash began speaking, the elevator came to a smooth stop, and the doors slid open to reveal a smiling family waiting on the other side.

I smiled tightly, and Ash followed me out of the elevator quietly. Once we heard those voices disappear into the elevator, she began again. "You're the one who said you didn't have a schedule and weren't in a hurry. You're the one who insisted on calling Jackson. Obviously, I can do whatever the hell I want, but I'd rather not get a lecture from my brother if I can avoid it."

We reached our room again, and I pulled out the card to

swipe it over the door sensor. It was this newfangled thing, some kind of circle pad instead of a slide, and it wouldn't work.

"Oh, for fuck's sake," I muttered to myself after the third time I'd tried it.

Ash elbowed me in the side and snatched the key card out of my hand. That little brush of contact—nothing more than her fingers against mine—was enough to send a hot sizzle of electricity spinning like fire through my arm.

"All you do is this." She held it over the pad, and the light magically turned green.

Rolling my eyes, I followed her into the room. Her bag fell to the floor, and she turned to look at me.

"Can you just not be an asshole? We'll make sure we get separate beds after this. Obviously, I can catch a hint. I know you'd rather be alone and not stuck with me," she said.

Oh, that fucking did it. I barely heard the thump of my bag on the floor as I closed the distance between us in one single stride. I spun her, pressing her against the wall beside us. "That's not the problem," I growled, right before claiming her mouth with mine.

Chapter Nine

ASH

Mack slanted his mouth over mine on the heels of a low growl. I gasped at the feel of him pressing against me, his strength surrounding me. The moment my lips opened under his, he muttered something into our kiss right before his tongue swept into my mouth.

I was wound so tight from pushing against the want and need spinning inside that it was glorious. The pure relief of finally giving in and pouring myself into this kiss was unlike anything I'd ever experienced.

Mack's big palm slid up to cradle my cheek as his other hand tangled roughly in my hair. The contrast of rough and gentle stirred the flames higher and higher. Our tongues twined roughly. This kiss was almost angry.

I'd never felt quite like this before—literally burning up with need. The startling acceptance of just how deeply my need for Mack ran was almost freeing in a strange way. I hadn't expected to want him, and I sure as hell hadn't expected to want him this fiercely, so I was wrestling with it inside myself.

It flew in the face of my careless promise to never want

another man. Certainly not Mack who I'd known as a little boy who got on my nerves. Certainly not one of my brother's oldest friends.

Mack growled again before he tore his mouth away from mine as roughly as the kiss began. We stared at each other, the sound of our breath coming in ragged heaves in the small entryway of the hotel room.

His dark blue eyes held mine. I could feel every beat of my heart echo down to my bones and the rush of blood in my ears.

I couldn't think past this very second with Mack—tall and strong, pressed against me, his arousal a hot brand at the apex of my thighs. I wasn't used to men towering over me. I was a tall girl, but with Mack, I felt small in the face of his immense size and strength. I felt invigorated, my body buzzing with awareness.

"*That's* the problem," Mack said, his voice low as he stared at me, the air charged around us as if lightning was about to strike and set the dry grass aflame.

"Why is that a problem?"

My question startled me, but I genuinely wanted to know the answer. Mack was a few years older than me, and I hadn't seen him in several years. But still, I knew his reputation. If I hadn't known him before Krista died, I might've thought he was an asshole. He wasn't quite known as a player. He was a guy who spun from one short-term relationship to the next, always making it crystal clear that he wanted nothing more than that. He could be cranky and irritable, but I knew behind that was something else, the boy who'd been so hurt when his sister died.

While I'd been wrestling with my own rampaging desire, or rather lust, for Mack, I couldn't deny a tiny part of me experienced a thrill at the thought he might want me. Mack was known as unattainable—the quiet, sexy, daring man who barely noticed anyone.

Mack stepped back abruptly, never once breaking his

gaze from mine. And *oh,* what a look it was. The blue of his eyes had darkened to navy. It was almost as if I could see the flames flickering in them.

"Are you serious?" he finally muttered in response to my question.

Mack's words and the twist of his lips when he spoke jolted me. It was as if someone had kicked me right back to a very familiar place inside. I knew what it was like not to be wanted. Oh, I knew that feeling so very well. Maybe there was some raw chemistry between us, but it was clear Mack wanted nothing to do with me. I pushed away from the wall, pressing the heel of my cowboy boot against it.

For a second, that put me close to Mack, but I moved away quickly, turning and striding across the room to look out over the parking lot. For a moment, my vision blurred, and it infuriated me to be on the verge of tears. I took a sharp breath and blinked hard until the tears passed. The Badlands were a dark silhouette in the distance, hulky in the night sky under the stars and the ethereal light of the moon.

I cast my reply to him over my shoulder, striving to keep my tone casual and dismissive. "Of course I was kidding."

Unfortunately for me, Mack knew me pretty well and seemed to sense my shaky mood. I heard him cross the room and stop at my side. When I let my eyes slide sideways, I saw his hands were stuffed in his pockets, and his eyes were concerned.

"Ash, I didn't mean—"

I cut him off quick. I didn't need one single person to feel bad or be worried about me and most certainly not Mack. "I don't know what you're about to say you didn't mean, but there's nothing to worry about. I'm fine. It was just a kiss. No need to get all worried that I want something from you. I don't. I won't get confused and think you want me."

"Ash," he began again.

This time, I spun away so fast I almost stumbled. Unfortunately, his hand landed on my shoulder, big and warm and sending a blast of heat straight through me. It dropped away when I shook it free and stalked across the room.

"Really, Mack," I said as I scooped my bag from the floor where it had fallen before Mack plastered me against the wall and kissed me senseless. Turning, I held his eyes as I crossed to the dresser and set my bag on top of it. "Just a kiss. Like I told you, I've sworn off men. That includes you. Let's call that a momentary lapse in judgment. Plus, you started it." I knew my tone had an edge to it.

The truth was, I was bitter about men. *Really* bitter. I could now add Mack to the long list of men who never wanted much from me.

This time, Mack seemed to have enough sense to keep his mouth shut. His eyes searched my face, and I gave a little shrug as if to punctuate my point. What that shrug actually meant was I didn't know what the hell I was doing. I didn't know why I wanted Mack, or why it cut so deeply to realize he didn't want me.

Just for once—even if it was a terrible idea—it would've been awfully nice for a man to get swept away by me. I unpacked my bag and then eyed the bed with my hands on my hips. We shifted into our typical routine. He took a shower first while I puttered around the room and found something to watch on TV.

While he showered, I called down to reception and had them bring up some extra pillows because I found only one extra one in the top of the closet. I brushed past Mack to take my own shower and wash off the sticky air from the bar hours earlier.

When I came out, the TV was off, and Mack already appeared to be asleep in the bed. He'd left a lamp on in the corner. I moved quietly over to my bag and put away my toiletries. I didn't care if it meant getting hot; I was sleeping in a sweatshirt and a pair of pants tonight. I needed layers of protection.

Curling onto my side with my back to Mack, I looked out the windows into the darkness. I idly counted the stars while I tried to stop feeling so fucking shitty inside. You could swear off men, but I'd learned the hard way that didn't mean you could convince yourself it wouldn't be nice for someone to want you enough.

"That's not necessary," Ash said over her shoulder, her tone sharp.

I stayed silent and followed her through the crowd. It had been a long few days. This was Ash's last show before the one in Niagara Falls. The tension between us had been building ever since that stupid kiss in the hotel.

I didn't exactly know how or why, but I knew I'd hurt her feelings. Not that I expected her to explain. She seemed to have taken the approach of staying cold and cranky with me most of the time. She pushed through a door into a back hallway. Since I'd started this trip with Ash, I'd learned that every bar had a back hallway where musicians and bands passing through would leave their gear. The hallways were usually narrow, and this one was no exception.

Ash acted as if I wasn't even behind her. It didn't matter, or that was what I told myself as I followed her. I was just being her friend. I told myself Jackson would expect me to keep an eye on her. In fact, he texted me just the other day to ask how she was doing and thanking me for sticking with her for the rest of this trip.

Jackson: I'm glad she's coming home, but I wasn't thrilled to hear she was trying to hitchhike by herself. For that alone, I owe you one. Any ETA yet?

Our detour in the Badlands had been cut short after that night. Ash had taken the tact of speaking to me as little as possible. I didn't know what the hell I'd done to piss her off so much. Maybe it was the kiss, but she'd made it clear she didn't want more. With anyone. I figured that meant we agreed it was a bad idea for anything to happen between us.

Ash swung her purse over her shoulder, and I picked up her guitar case before she yanked it right out of my hands. "I have this, Mack. You sure you don't wanna let me just borrow your truck for the rest of the trip?" Her chin was set in a mulish line as her eyes met mine.

"I thought we already had this conversation," I replied.

"Right. You think Jackson wants you to keep me company. Whatever. I have two places booked in Niagara Falls, and then one more in Kentucky. We can manage that, right?"

"Of course."

I knew I could handle it, but that didn't mean it wouldn't suck. It was bad enough I had to fend off my fierce lust for Ash, but I felt even worse knowing I'd somehow hurt her feelings. Piling on top of that was my muddled confusion about all of it. Because, what the hell? I didn't make a habit of worrying about *feelings*.

Ever since I'd encountered Ash, it felt as if she tilted the axis of my world slightly. Not much made sense. I only knew one thing for certain. I wanted her to the point of madness.

———

A day later, we crossed into Upstate New York. Although it was summer, the air felt crisper here than I knew it would in the South. Traffic began to pick up as we approached

Niagara Falls. It was a world-renowned tourist destination, so that wasn't exactly a surprise.

Ash looked over at me. "Do you have a passport?" she asked, the first friendly question she'd voluntarily offered in days at this point.

"I do. Why do you ask?"

"My show isn't until tomorrow night. It's on the US side, but I always heard the view of the Falls is better on the Canadian side. Do you want to cross over?"

"We're here. We might as well cross the border."

A few hours later, we stood and watched the Falls. The rush of the water was so profound I could feel it vibrating in every cell in my body.

Ash finally snapped out of her funk. "It's amazing," she called. Her words were caught on the wind and almost lost in the roar of the water.

With the place teeming with visitors, I understood why Niagara Falls was considered one of the Seven Wonders of the World. No amount of crowds or tacky touristy signs could drown out the stunning power and beauty of them. Ash and I watched for as long as we could before another group came along, and we had to move to make room for the view.

Even as we walked back to my truck, you could hear them in the distance. I watched the river by the road, rushing with its momentum already picking up.

Ash stopped at one point, her brown hair catching and swirling in the wind. "Thank you."

I looked straight into her gaze, and my heart gave a resounding kick. "Thank you for suggesting we come over to this side. I'm sure the US side is good too, but this was incredible."

"Pictures don't do it justice," Ash said, her eyes shining.

"Definitely not."

We climbed back in my truck, drove back into the US, and found a hotel. Although my body still buzzed with need when I got too close to Ash, the cold tension that had been hanging over her seemed to have dissipated with our visit to the Falls. For that, I was relieved.

We ordered dinner at a diner and called Jackson together at Ash's suggestion. Things felt as comfortable as they could be between us by the time we retired to our separate beds in the hotel room.

Chapter Eleven

MACK

There was a blinding flash out of the corner of my eye followed by a loud crunching sound. I felt more than saw the collision. Ash let out a startled squeak.

Acting on instinct, I swung my truck along the shoulder and came to a jerking stop. Glancing across the highway, I saw flames flickering from under the hood of one car with another spinning before it flipped and skidded into the guardrail.

After throwing my seat belt off, I jumped out. Other cars had stopped on the highway. Scanning the two vehicles, I saw that the driver of the one on fire was already out and racing around to the other side of the vehicle.

Ash was right behind me. We ran together to the vehicle with the fire. Time was all we had on our side. I looked into the back of the car to see a baby in a car seat. The driver was out and clearly fine, but he was struggling to get the back passenger door open.

I silently cursed. Time graced us with its blessing, and inside of a minute, we got the baby out. After handing over the baby in the car seat to Ash and confirming no one else was in the vehicle, I looked at her and the man who'd been driving. "Get to the other side of the highway. The fire can catch fast, so don't wait."

As soon as they were on their way, I ran to check on the other vehicle, which had overturned and was crushed against the guardrail.

Peering inside, I saw that the driver was conscious and seemed okay enough to be turning his head to look at me. "You okay?" I asked.

"I think so," the man replied, his voice coming out slow. Both of us looked toward the passenger together. The woman had a trickle of blood running down from her hairline in front of her ear.

"Sarah," the man said.

The passenger side window was shattered, so I reached through and rested my fingers over her pulse. The woman's pulse was thready but definitely there.

"How do you feel?" I asked the man.

"I just need to know if Sarah's okay," he said, his tone understandably worried.

"She's got a pulse, so that's good. I'm Mack. Although I'm not on duty and I don't live here, I'm a first responder and a firefighter. If you think you're okay to move, let's see if we can get you out on your side. I can't tell from here, but you might even be able to open your door."

"What about Sarah?" the man asked.

"I'd prefer not to move her until an emergency vehicle gets here. That way, they can get her stabilized right away, depending on what's going on."

Peering in through the window, I could see the woman's lower legs were bent at an awkward angle from where the door got crushed when it spun against the guardrail. Looking back at the man who hadn't moved yet, I added, "I'll come around there."

The passenger side of the vehicle had taken the brunt of the blow. That side of the roof must've struck the pavement when the car flipped. Rounding the other side of the car, I carefully tested the door handle. "It's probably going to make a god-awful sound," I said, looking at the man, "but I think it'll open. You ready?"

The man reached for his seat belt, but I shook my head. "Not yet. Let me get this open first. What's your name, by the way?"

"Dan."

He turned to look at Sarah again. "Sarah, can you hear me?"

"Let's get you out first."

A loud scraping sound where the frame was bent made it a challenge to open the door, but I was able to open the door with a strong pull. With my help, Dan clambered out, and by all accounts, he appeared fine. "You're probably gonna be sore as hell tomorrow from the impact and bruises you're not aware of yet, but so far, you're looking good," I commented.

Dan nodded. "Can we pull Sarah out?"

Straightening, I looked down the highway, disappointed not to see any sign of an emergency vehicle yet. Just then, the flames took hold on the other car. Sparks landed on the pavement, igniting a trail of fluid leaking from this car. In a matter of seconds, flames were licking along the side of the car.

We couldn't afford to wait. Racing around the car, I reached through the window and pulled Sarah out. She remained unconscious, so I lifted her carefully and cradled her in my arms, walking swiftly to get clear of the vehicle in case the flames exploded when they reached the gas tank.

The interstate highway had a wide median in the center. With help from Dan, we eased her down on the grass just as several emergency vehicles arrived on the scene.

I heard a loud blast and figured the gas tank had caught fire. Immediately on the heels of that, I heard a startled cry, and every hair on my body stood. Despite the commotion around us, I knew that was Ash's voice.

With my heart practically leaping out of my chest, I stood and spun around, my eyes scanning the area until I saw her stumbling backward. The emergency crews were moving into gear with the fire truck immediately focusing on the fire and the EMTs hurrying over the guardrail with a stretcher. Catching the eye of a woman on the crew, I barked, "She has a pulse. We had to get her out because the car was catching fire."

I didn't wait for a reply before I raced toward Ash. I reached her side just as she eased her hips down onto the guardrail. "What the hell happened?" I asked when I stopped in front of her, climbing over the railing so I could kneel beside her.

She was cradling her arm, and I reflexively reached for it. Gently holding her elbow, I pulled her hand away to see the singed fabric of her blouse. "What happened?" I repeated.

"I don't know. When the car exploded, something flew through the air and hit me." Ash's words came out slowly. Her eyes were wide when she looked down at her arm and then back at me.

"Can I take a look?" I asked.

She nodded, clearly still stunned enough that she wasn't even really reacting.

After carefully pulling the fabric apart, I saw that she had a burn mark and nothing more. Fortunately, whatever hit her must've bounced off after leaving behind a minor burn on her forearm. "This will be annoying, but I would guess the bruising tomorrow might be more painful," I commented.

Looking back up, I lifted a hand and captured the hair falling over her eyes to brush it out of the way. "You're going to be fine. It looks like something just glanced off your arm. It doesn't look worse than a first-degree burn. How do you feel?"

"It just scared me. That's all. It hit really hard."

"I bet." I looked away to see small burning bits scattered over the highway. Any one of them could've been the culprit. Bringing my focus back to Ash, I tried to will the tightness in my chest to ease. I'd been calm all through this because I was trained to stay composed when the shit hit the fan. But this was Ash. Even though objectively, I knew she was okay, I was having an intense reaction to even the threat of harm to her.

When I looked back at her, her eyes held mine, fear flickering in them. I wanted to fold her into my arms.

"Excuse me, sir," a voice said.

"Yeah?" I said as I straightened, keeping a hand on Ash's shoulder. I couldn't bring myself not to touch her at this moment.

"I understand you got that woman out of the car? Good work and just in time," one of the emergency workers said.

"No problem. I'm a first responder. We just happened to be driving by. Normally, I would've waited, but we didn't have time with the fire. Is she conscious yet?"

"Yeah. Looks like she'll be okay. She sustained a broken ankle, and the cut on her forehead will require a few stitches. She took a hit to her head, but she's oriented. Dan, her husband, was hoping to talk to you before we leave with her."

I looked down toward Ash. "Go ahead," she said. "I'm fine."

"Can you take a look at the burn on her arm?" I asked as I stepped over the guardrail to approach Dan where he was standing beside the stretcher as they prepped it to lift into the ambulance.

"Absolutely," the woman said quickly.

"Thank you." Dan held my eyes when I stopped in front of him. "They're telling me if you hadn't gotten her out of the car, well... I don't even wanna think about it," he rushed out.

"No need because that's not how it went. If I hadn't been here, somebody else would've helped," I replied.

"Thank you," he repeated.

A jumble of activity followed with the police gathering statements from everybody who witnessed the accident. The highway was closed off while they cleaned up the debris. It was a good hour before we were cleared to leave.

Ash had the emergency tech cut off her burned sleeve. A light bandage was placed over the burn itself after they cleaned it. Once we were back in my truck, I glanced over. "How ya doing?"

Ash still looked shaken, but she shrugged. "Well, that was just crazy. I'm glad everyone's okay."

"Are *you* okay?" I pressed.

At her nod, I started the truck. I still hadn't been able to grab the steely anchor of calm I was accustomed to after events like this.

The last time someone I personally knew had been in an emergency, everything went wrong. I'd been there and hadn't been able to do one single thing to save her. I knew that was part of what had me so unsettled. Yet I didn't know what the hell to do with how much I wanted to wrap Ash in my arms and hold her close. I knew that instinct wasn't simply about protecting her. There was something akin to a craving inside me.

At that moment, her stomach growled, and she slapped her hand over it with a startled laugh. "We were supposed to stop and get brunch," she commented.

Chapter Twelve

ASH

Dragging my sleeve across my face to wipe off the sheen of sweat gathered there, I walked across the stage, the sound of the last chord still reverberating through my body. The small bar was packed, and the sound of the crowd filled the space.

I was jostled on one side as I walked down the stairs. A piercing whistle elicited an involuntary flinch as I tried to make my way through the crowded area to the side of the stage.

"Hey, gorgeous! Fucking listen when somebody tells you you're hot!" The man's angry voice had an edge to it that made me uncomfortable. I hugged my guitar to the front of my body, but that turned out to be a mistake. It exposed my back, and the next thing I knew, a hand was squeezing my ass.

"Hey!" I spun around, reflexively swinging my hand in the direction of wherever that hand came from.

"Get your fucking hands off her." Mack's voice, low and authoritative, sliced through the noise around me.

I felt him before I saw him. His presence was potent and large. The second I felt him approach from behind, a sense of relief rolled through me. I'd been on edge all evening. I told myself the internal tumult from the accident would only feed my songs tonight. That had been true, yet it didn't help me deal with the annoying side effects of playing music live.

I loved to play, and it was my personal touchstone no matter what was going on. Any musician who was halfway decent wouldn't turn their nose up at getting big and famous, yet that absolutely wasn't what drove me to play. I enjoyed the quaint bars. The connection I had with the audience felt more personal.

Except I hated this part. Mack's arm came around my shoulders. "Back off," he said when another guy made a comment I could barely hear, only catching a part of the man's next comment at the tail end. "...her sweet ass."

"You fucker." Before I even realized what was happening, Mack's arm slid off my shoulder, and he had the guy's shirt bunched in his fist right at the throat as he lifted him off the ground.

"What the fuck?!" the man snarled although he was pretty helpless at the moment.

"Back off and don't talk trash," Mack said, tossing the guy away as if he were nothing more than a lightweight bag of trash.

His strong arm wrapped around my shoulders again, and then he guided me through the crowd with ease. People tended to get out of the way for Mack, and I didn't blame them. He was big, and he had a forbidding edge to him with his broad shoulders and the fact he stood taller than most men at six feet five inches.

In another moment, Mack was holding the door open to the back hallway. The sounds of the crowd muted behind us just as the act that followed me began their set.

"You okay?" Mack asked as I turned and sagged against the wall.

"Yeah, I'm fine." When I looked up into Mack's eyes, navy and liquid, my heart executed a disorienting flip in my chest. I didn't know what it was about Mack, but the sense of protectiveness he exuded was intoxicating.

It also turned me on. Although, of late, all Mack had to do was exist in the same space with me, and I was turned on. Still unsettled from dealing with the accident earlier, I couldn't seem to think clearly.

"Let's go," I said, pushing away from the wall.

Just then, the back door swung open again. It hit me in the shoulder, and I stumbled slightly. Mack caught me, his hand landing right on my hip when he steadied me. "Easy there," he murmured.

"Oh, sorry," the woman who'd just come hurrying through chirped. She was one of the waitresses for the bar.

"No problem," I said as I reflexively turned into the shelter of Mack's embrace as his arm curled around my shoulders again. God, he smelled *soooo* good. I could smell a hint of fresh soap from the shower he took at the hotel before we came out. Underneath was the slight crisp scent he carried no matter what.

She looked back and forth between us quickly and smiled. "Your girlfriend's voice is incredible," she said, addressing Mack.

"I know."

His choice not to correct her perception that I was his girlfriend sent an unexpected shiver chasing over my skin. She gave us a quick wave and hurried down the hallway. Moments later, I had my purse and Mack was carrying my guitar when we stepped out into the parking lot.

"Hungry?" he asked with a slight lift of his chin, a subtle gesture he did often when he was asking a question.

"Course I'm hungry. I'm always hungry after I play."

Mack's responding slow smile had butterflies bursting to life in my belly.

"Then let's go get you fed."

———

"I got it," Mack said when he reached for the check the waitress had placed in the middle of the table.

Right as I curled my two fingers around the edge of the small slip of paper, his big palm landed on top of mine. My pulse stuttered and then lunged. Apparently, even a simple innocent touch from him made my body spark like a firecracker. That was the effect Mack was having on me day after day after day.

I looked up into his gaze and cast a glare at him. "I got it," I said, stubbornly tossing his words right back at him.

"You're not really gonna argue with me about this, are you?"

He didn't move his hand, and his touch was sending licks of fire over my skin, and my breath was getting shallow. Yanking my hand out from under his, I rolled my eyes, striving to play it cool. When cool was the opposite of how I felt.

"Not worth the fight."

As he pulled his wallet out, I couldn't help but look at his hands. They were big, like all of him, yet they were almost elegant. His fingers were long and nimble. I could only imagine how his hands would feel on my body.

Stop it!

Oh, stop being so prissy. You want Mack, and he wants you. I dare you to do something about it.

Shut up.

I wanted to make my critical, ever taunting voice die a quick death inside my brain.

It doesn't matter if I want Mack; he's made it clear it's not a good call.

Says who? Mack is nothing like Kyle and Brian.

Oh, Jesus Christ. Shut the hell up.

I did not need to be thinking about how I knew Mack would never treat any woman as carelessly as Kyle did, or how he would never cheat on someone the way Brian did for months before our wedding.

Sometimes, I wondered if other people had so many competing internal opinions taking up space and time in their minds.

Our waitress took the cash from Mack when he held it up as she hurried by. "Be right back with your change," she called over her shoulder.

Mack leaned back in his seat. "We've eaten at a lot of diners over the past few weeks. Have a favorite?"

"Hmm." I cocked my head to the side, drumming my fingertips on the table. "Let me think about it. We should have a vote."

"A vote with just the two of us?" His lips kicked up at one corner, and those unsettled butterflies took flight again, tickling the inside of my belly.

I shrugged. "Maybe. Maybe we'll agree. Or maybe not. I know my favorite was that place in the Badlands."

"Seriously? That's my favorite. It was damn good."

"I love the name too," I added.

"I don't even remember the name. What was it?" Mack countered.

"Diner. That was it."

Mack's slow grin was like a spur in the flanks of my pulse, and it obediently kicked up to a faster gallop.

"They kept it simple," I managed, my voice coming out a little breathy. Dear God. I couldn't even discuss restaurants with him without getting stupid.

The waitress dropped off Mack's change, and he left a generous tip. That was something I liked about him. He wasn't cheap. Kyle had been so freaking cheap, always nitpicking and leaving shitty tips. Waitressing wasn't the greatest job. I'd done it for years in college, so I was big on tipping well.

While Mack put the rest of the change into his wallet, he looked over at me. His gaze was like a tractor beam. Once I was caught within it, I couldn't look away. "You doing okay?" he asked.

"I'm fine," I said quickly.

"I know you're fine, but that accident was kind of intense. How's your arm feeling?"

I pushed up the sleeve of my thin cotton blouse and studied the lightweight bandage on my forearm. "It's fine. The soreness is settling in, though, like you said it would. Are you okay?"

"Of course."

Although neither one of us said another word for a moment, or maybe two, something passed between us, and the air snapped and crackled with energy. This thing with us seemed to have a life of its own.

Chapter Thirteen

MACK

Although the hotel where we were staying was maybe only two miles from the diner, the distance felt much longer. I'd been trying to keep a leash on this rampaging need for Ash, and I was definitely losing my grip.

Something about today had set everything in motion inside me. The latch on the gate had been knocked loose. Not only had it swung open but it'd also been blown off the hinges. I was accustomed to the rush of adrenaline that carried me through an emergency. It was my job to remain steady when everything else was out of control. Today's emergency wasn't even that big of a deal, all things considered.

That wasn't to say it hadn't been terrifying for the people directly affected. For me, only one slice in time kept replaying—the sound of Ash's cry.

She was fine. Hell, she was so fine she went on to play tonight after we checked in at the hotel. She'd shrugged it off when I asked her if she felt up to it. She pointed out it was her left arm, and she was right handed. She changed her clothes and insisted on keeping the gig. It didn't matter to me that she appeared *fine* on the surface. That tiny event triggered something inside me.

A distant corner of my mind knew precisely what it was. Only one other event had involved someone who mattered to me like that. I only had one sister left now because my other sister was dead.

No matter what became of this chemistry brewing between us, Ash had been my friend for years and was closely tied to so many people I cared about. Even if I tried to tell myself she wasn't that important, it was a bald-faced lie.

It had been over fourteen years since Krista died, yet every single detail about that event was carved in stone in my mind. It wasn't my fault. I *knew* this. Another thing I knew was that the heart didn't listen very well to logic and reason. I still felt guilty. I'd been there. I'd replayed that afternoon so many times, trying to figure out what I could've changed in the series of events that ended in her death, but I always came up with the same answer. Nothing.

My mind shied away from going down that well-worn path, immediately colliding with my inconvenient desire when Ash spoke.

"You just missed the hotel," she said, a low, husky laugh following.

Hitting the brakes and my blinker, I turned quickly into a gas station parking lot to go back. "Sorry, totally spaced out."

I slid my eyes sideways to run right into Ash's gaze. Eyes. In all of the years I'd known her, I hadn't thought much about her eyes. I sure as hell hadn't thought they were *fuck-me* eyes.

They totally were. That blue darkened every time we looked at each other. She had thick brown eyelashes that framed her eyes, illuminating the blue. She didn't wear makeup, never had that I could recall, and she certainly had no need for it. Her gorgeous eyes tilted up at the corners, and her cheekbones angled down to her kissable lips.

I almost missed the turn. Again. This time, I wasn't lost in my thoughts, but in her gaze instead. My heart felt like it had been jump-started, rusty from years of inaction. Honestly, I couldn't say I'd ever let any woman matter to me in a romantic sense. I wasn't an asshole; I just wasn't interested in frilly things like romance. A few hours between the sheets and a friendly parting were more than enough. Or so I had convinced myself.

Ash broke the stare down between us, her breath escaping in a puff when she turned away to look out the window. During the next minute or two, the small space in my truck was tense. It felt as if lightning might strike between us. We definitely needed to run for cover, but there was nowhere to go.

I parked, and we walked in silence through the lobby. The ride up in the elevator was quiet. My pulse kept racing along. Something had to give. This trip couldn't end soon enough.

When we got to the room, every sound grated on me. It was like all my nerves were exposed to the air, and only one thing could soothe them.

"I just need to go to the bathroom, then you can have the shower," Ash said as she dropped her purse on the dresser and practically ran into the bathroom.

Even though I had showered this afternoon after our rescue event, going to the bars usually left me reeking of smoke and beer and sweat from the crowd. Ash told me every single night she played that I didn't have to go to the shows. But I couldn't *not* go. Listening to her sing and strum her guitar was like peering into her soul. One thing I'd figured out since our worlds had collided was that Ash was far more guarded than she used to be. She used to be more open and easygoing. Now, when she played, a thin layer of protection shimmered around her.

I craved hearing her sing on an almost elemental level. Leaning back on the bed, I let out a sigh.

After she came out, I took a quick shower and refused to give in to finding my own release. It didn't feel right now, and she was just outside the door and wide-awake. When I stepped through the door while I was toweling my hair to find her in the middle of changing, I forgot every single reason we shouldn't act on this crazy mad lust between us.

Ash stood there beside the dresser in a tank top and her panties. Hot pink panties. Maybe ten feet separated us where I stood just beyond the bathroom door. It felt as if an electrical current flickered in the air between us.

The paisley cotton blouse she'd been wearing earlier over the tank top slipped from her fingertips to the floor, landing in a rumple at her feet. Her brown hair fell in a tousle around her shoulders, doing nothing to mask her tight nipples pressing against her thin cotton tank top.

My breath came out in a hiss between my teeth as the towel dropped from my hand. In several strides, I was standing in front of her.

Ash looked up at me, her mouth parting and her tongue darting out to moisten her plump bottom lip. "That was fast," she whispered.

Inanely, I asked, "What was fast?"

Her throat worked in a swallow. "Your shower."

I nodded. I didn't know what I meant to do, but I couldn't bring myself to move away from her, and my hands literally itched to touch her. I searched her eyes, almost as if I could find the answer of what to do there.

"What do you want, Mack?" Ash whispered.

"You."

That one syllable, forming a single word, encapsulated everything I'd been trying to avoid ever since my path inter-sected with hers weeks ago. My entire body felt as if it were about to burst at the seams. The need I'd been trying to contain was burgeoning and growing, its force and intensity well beyond my control and discipline.

Ash's breath caught in her throat, and I could see the rapid flutter of her pulse along the side of her neck.

"I thought you said that was a problem." Her words came out slow and raspy.

"Sugar, it is, but I'm tired of trying to fight it." It was a relief to speak the truth.

Ash's eyes widened slightly, and then she bit her lip. Jesus. I was jealous of her teeth.

"What do you want?" I asked.

I might be crazy and stupid to act on this, but it was imperative that I knew Ash wanted it too. Because if she didn't, that was all I would need to get a grip.

Her eyes searched mine, darkening as we stared at each other. The air was heavy, loaded with the charge bouncing between us. My heart pounded hard and fast as I waited for her answer. For the first time ever, at least when it came to a woman, I experienced a flicker of uncertainty. Perhaps I'd misread Ash. I mentally shied away from the emotional implications of that.

"You," she replied, mirroring my answer.

That was all I needed. I let the reins slip through my fingers as I finally, fucking *finally*, closed the distance between us. I stepped to within an inch of her. I could feel the heat emanating from her, and her scent wrapped itself around me. Having shared up close and personal space with her for weeks now, her scent was maddening. She smelled subtly sweet, and I wanted to eat her up.

My hand was almost shaking as I lifted it to catch one of the loose curls that hung down alongside her breast. My knuckle brushed that sweet curve, and the sensation sent electricity zipping through me, almost burning me.

Ash's breasts pressed against my chest when she took a deep breath. I could see the trepidation I felt reflected in her eyes. Maybe this was crazy, maybe it was a terrible idea, but this desire wasn't going anywhere. The pressure of it was building and building and building, and there was only one release valve.

"Are you sure about this?" I heard myself asking.

She looked back at me quietly. "Not really. But I can't stop wanting you. It's just getting worse."

Her honesty nearly undid me. "Exactly," I rasped.

Chapter Fourteen

MACK

Just before I dipped my head and claimed her mouth, Ash placed her hand on my bare chest, right over my heart. It leaped toward her touch, almost as if it recognized the source of my muddled uncertainty, confusion, and *absolute* desire and need.

She dipped her head and leaned forward, her lips landing at the juncture between my collarbones, pressing a warm and soft kiss in the divot there. That subtle touch was like a brand, sizzling through my skin, the heat of it spiraling into the lust drumming through my body.

And then my hand was sliding into her hair and tangling in the silky strands. I cupped her nape, angled her head to the side, and fit my mouth over hers. She let out a soft moan the moment our lips collided, her mouth opening to invite my tongue inside. The relief of finally kissing her again was acute.

Our kiss was an instant conflagration. Ash arched up into me, pressing her soft, supple body against mine. Having her in my arms was a dizzying form of heaven. I simultaneously wanted all of her at once while trying to frantically absorb every sensation and not miss a single second of this, of her.

Kissing her was madness—a sensual twining of our tongues. My teeth finally got to assuage their earlier envy when I drew away and nipped at her bottom lip before diving back in. One of her hands slid slowly over my chest while the other slipped around my neck, and her fingers teased my hair.

My arousal was insistent. I was so hard that I ached. Untangling my fingers from her hair, I slipped my hand down her back to cup her bottom, letting out a rough groan when she rocked her hips into me. I needed *more*, and I needed more *now*.

With a growl, I broke free from our kiss. I lifted her against me, a wave of satisfaction crashing through me when she curled her long legs around my hips, and I could feel the heat of her arousal pressing against my cock. Turning, I took two strides until we reached one of the beds, and I lowered her hips on it.

I was struggling with a unique problem. I wanted her so badly, I almost couldn't bear not to be plastered against her. Yet I didn't want this to be a rushed coupling that would do little to slake the ferocity of my need for her.

As I eased her on the bed, a piercing sense of missing the feel of her against me struck me hard when I rested my hands on either side of her hips. When our gazes collided, my heart started jackhammering again, and I lost my breath. She snatched it right out of me with the look in her eyes— dark, stormy, and sultry.

Lifting a hand, I trailed my knuckles lightly over her collarbone. "Beautiful," I murmured.

Ash held still, watching me quietly. I let my fingertips trace along the curve of her tank top before lightly cupping a breast, loving how her nipple puckered even tighter when I teased it with my thumb. I couldn't resist and leaned forward to close my mouth over it, right through the cotton.

She gasped sharply, arching up into me. The weight of her breast felt *so* good in my palm. I let my teeth graze lightly over her nipple as I drew back. "Ash," I said, my tone reverent. My voice was rough on the edges, my need having worn down any effort to speak clearly.

Ash curled her fingers around the hem of her tank top and lifted it off in one swooping arc. It fell to the side of the bed. I'd been up close and personal with Ash for weeks now, but I hadn't seen her naked. The sight of her caught me by the throat and seized my lungs again.

Ash was tall but curvy. She didn't have a bra on, and her breasts tumbled loose, her nipples a deep, dusky pink. My breath finally came out in a tortured groan. My hands fell to either side of her hips again with my head dropping into the crook of her neck.

"Damn, Ash. You're not supposed to be this fucking sexy."

Ash murmured something I didn't catch. Leaning back, I asked, "What did you say?"

Her lips were puffy from our kisses, her cheeks flushed, and her hair in a wild tangle around her shoulders. She literally took my breath away. I was no stranger to sex, but the fierceness of my need for Ash was unfamiliar. Our need was almost a separate force shimmering around us.

She didn't say anything, but I saw uncertainty flickering in her eyes, and she shrugged. I filed that away. Somebody had done a number on her. Anger blazed through me, but I didn't linger on it, and the feeling only spun into the rest of the storm thrashing inside me.

"Don't think. I'm an expert on these matters," I said, managing to lighten my tone.

Ash's lips kicked up in a slight smile. "Are you now?" she teased in return.

"You know it."

Ash licked her lips, and I couldn't resist leaning forward

to kiss her again, letting my tongue tease with hers before drawing back.

"You're so beautiful and so sexy I can hardly stand it." I punctuated that statement with another long kiss. Lifting my head, I held her gaze. "Now, sugar, I'm going to make you forget everything."

"Do your best," Ash challenged.

That little comment was something she used to say all the time when we were kids and dared each other to do whatever ridiculously scary thing we'd concocted. Although lust was laying claim to my body at this moment, my heart gave a funny little tumble in response.

Ash and I had history. Lots of it. Jackson would fucking kill me if he knew what was happening right now, yet I couldn't even summon the energy nor the will to give a damn.

I dusted kisses along the side of her neck, loving the feel of her goose bumps rising on her skin. I savored the plush weight of her breasts in my hands. I let my palm glide over the soft curve of her belly and lower, a growl of satisfaction coming from my throat when I encountered the drenched cotton between her thighs.

"Somebody's all wet," I murmured as I drew my lips away from her nipple yet again. Because I couldn't fucking get enough of her nipples and the way she arched into me every time I caught them with my lips and nipped. Ash seemed to enjoy the edge of pain.

"It's all your fault," Ash murmured between ragged breaths. "It was bad enough before you kissed me, and then you kissed me."

Her tone was accusatory, and I lifted my head, letting my eyes drift over her face and down her body. Fuck me. Ash was wearing nothing but a pair of pink cotton panties sitting on the edge of the bed with her knees splayed and her breasts rising and falling with each heaving breath. She had a flush of passion all over her skin, and her eyes were dark and wide. She looked thoroughly kissed. I needed more.

"It's all your fault, sugar," I countered.

"I don't think so. You're the one who kissed me first."

"Whatever. Back to my point, you're too damn sexy. I've been cooped up with you for weeks, and I can't take it anymore."

I hooked a finger over the edge of her panties and delved into her slick, swollen folds. "I need these off," I muttered.

I didn't even want to take my fingers out of her sweet, hot core, but I had bigger plans, and her panties were in the way.

Ash lifted her hips as I tugged them off. When I looked down, and my eyes landed on her pink and glistening pussy, my knees nearly gave out.

"You're wearing too many clothes," she gasped. Her words ended on a moan when I tugged her hips closer to the edge of the bed and brought my fingers right where they needed to be.

"In a minute," I murmured in reply. Then I was kneeling and pressing her thighs apart. I dropped kisses on the insides of her thighs, satisfaction washing through me at the way she shivered and trembled under my touch.

By the time my mouth made it to her center, Ash had one hand gripping my hair and the other clutching the bedspread in her fist. I teased my fingers through her arousal, circling my thumb over her clit before finally bowing my head and tasting her.

She was sweet with a hint of tang. Her sharp cry punctuated a long, low moan. I explored every inch of her pussy until I felt her tightening and her channel rippling around my fingers. Only then did I bring my tongue to swirl around her clit again and give it the slightest bit of suction. She came apart with a ragged cry, her entire body trembling as her pussy clamped around my fingers.

I needed inside her. *Now*.

Rising, I kicked off my shorts and pulled her hips closer to the edge of the bed again. My cock was aching and hard in my fist as I gripped it. I was just about to bury myself inside her when I realized I needed a condom.

"Fuck," I muttered as I swung away quickly, striding to find my wallet. A few bills fell to the floor when I yanked out a condom and returned to the bed.

I had it on in a hot second. Ash's legs were already curling around my hips when I forced myself to hold still. I didn't know why, but I needed to see her face when I filled her.

With the crown of my cock resting at her entrance, teased by the kiss of her arousal, I lifted my head. "Ash."

Her dark lashes swept up. Although everything about this was bordering on the edge of insanity and driven by raw lust, when I reached to brush her sweat-dampened hair off her cheek, an acute sense of gentleness gusted through me like a soft breeze. It wasn't an emotion I was familiar with, and it twined like a vine around everything else I was feeling.

"What?" she asked, her question a ragged whisper.

"I need to see you." Even my answer surprised me because it was honest and unvarnished.

Sex was just sex, or so I told myself every single time I'd had it before. Including the very first time when I lost my virginity to an older girl in high school. I'd always believed it was a choice to ascribe any more meaning to it. I hadn't realized how thoroughly I'd absorbed that belief until Ash.

"I need to see you," I repeated as she stared back at me.

With every breath, Ash's breasts pressed against my chest. We were plastered together with her on the edge of the bed and me gripping the side of her hip with one hand and cradling her cheek in the other.

I nudged at her entrance, breaching the very core of her slightly. On another breath, I slid all the way home into her silky, clenching sheath.

"Oh, God," I muttered, my words actually slurring.

Her eyes widened when I settled in deeper. I stared into her gaze, watching the color darken and her lips part on a soft gasp. I couldn't think over the drumming of my heart.

Chapter Fifteen

ASH

My pulse thundered through every cell in my body, and all of my focus zeroed in on where I was joined with Mack. I looked up into his face, his liquid blue eyes. Mack was an intense man all on his own.

But being this close to him overpowered everything else until there was nothing but him, and us, and this moment. He invaded and permeated every part of my body, taking over my senses and holding me captive.

Given how big he was everywhere else, it didn't surprise me that Mack was well endowed, but it was... much. Enough that there'd been a subtle burn when he stretched and filled me. He held still as my body adjusted to him. One of his hands gripped my hip tightly, and the feel of his fingers digging into my skin felt so good.

Everything felt beyond good. His hard, muscled chest, the light abrasion from the dusting of his hair against my breasts, strong muscular thighs where they rested between mine. One of his hands cradled my cheek, his touch almost gentle and making me feel things I didn't want to feel. I was *made* of sensation.

He drew back slowly and then sank in again, asking, "Is this okay?"

Although the question was polite, his words were rough with a hint of dirty to them.

"Oh God, yes." I let out a rough moan as he drew back and filled me again.

His low chuckle sent a prickle down my spine, and then his hand tangled in my hair as he began to fuck me, hard. I needed it that way, hard and fast.

He met me stroke for stroke as I arched to flex against him. My orgasm raced toward me rapidly. The friction was just right where we were joined as he held my hips in place with each stroke. The pleasure swirled faster and faster inside like a wheel about to spin loose. It finally reached a breaking point and snapped free. Pleasure scattered like sparks through my body as I shuddered roughly against him.

Mack followed me over the edge almost instantly, his hand tightening in my hair to the point that my scalp stung. I savored the burn of it in the relief of my own pleasure. I heard him cry my name in a rough shout over the thundering of my heart as the waves of pleasure slowed into eddies and ripples. Before I could even catch my breath, Mack was lifting me and striding into the bathroom with me in his arms.

––––––––

I had to pee. With the insistent pressure in my bladder finally dragging me out of my sleep, I felt the warmth of Mack cocooning me. Good lord, he was a big man. His presence was like a giant bear in the bed with me—a muscled, sexy, hot bear I wanted to lick all over. Again.

Our hotel room was dark. Opening my eyes, I was facing the empty bed I hadn't slept in last night, and I didn't want to get up. It felt good—oh, so deliciously good—to be held in Mack's warm embrace. I'd discovered last night that he was a cuddler.

My bladder repeated its protest, so I slid carefully out of his arms. I was afraid he'd wake up, and the reality of what we'd done last night would come crashing over both of us. I wasn't ready for reality to poke its way into this scene yet.

I tiptoed across the carpet and scurried into the bathroom. I was relieved the door closed soundlessly. I took care of business and held my breath when I flushed the toilet. Flicking on the light over the mirror, I took stock.

My hair was messy, and my lips were still swollen from our endless kisses last night. It hadn't ended after the first round in the bed. After he carried me into the shower, the kisses began all over again while the hot water rained down around us, and Mack's nimble fingers teased me to another breathless climax. Then I took him in my mouth, gratified when his fingers gripped my hair and he cried my name in a growl as he came.

Staring at myself in the mirror, I realized I looked like a woman who'd been thoroughly fucked. Oh, how my ego needed that. Closing my eyes, I took a deep breath. When I let it out in a soft sigh, I turned out the light. No matter what happened now, at least I'd felt like the center of a man's world for one night and maybe it wasn't such an impossible feat for a man to lose himself in me.

Swinging the door open quietly, I tiptoed back to bed, relieved to hear Mack's breath still coming in steady, even gusts. I slid carefully under the covers, holding my breath as I hoped not to wake him. He'd rolled onto his back while I'd been in the bathroom, and I was a little bit disappointed. I didn't know a trick to gracefully get him to spoon me again, so I gingerly pulled the covers up and tried to relax.

After a moment, I heard him mumble something and then roll toward me, his arm coming around me. His hand landed just under one of my breasts, and my nipples perked up shamelessly.

"Where'd you go?" he murmured, his voice slurred and frayed from sleep.

"Bathroom," I whispered.

My lips were curling into a smile. Hell, it felt like my entire body was smiling.

"Mmm." He dragged me closer to him effortlessly.

Even half-asleep, Mack's strength easily pulled me against him. My knee hitched over his thigh as I curled into the crook of his shoulder.

"There," he murmured. I felt his lips press a kiss against my hair as his big palm smoothed down my side and came to rest cupping my bottom.

My body was already responding with arousal, a little spin of heat shimmying through me. Mack murmured something unintelligible before his breath instantly shifted back into sleep.

In my whatever relationship with Kyle, he was not a cuddly guy. My ex-fiancé hadn't been either. With my heart smiling along with every other cell in my body, I didn't know what to think of just how much I *loved* the way Mack held me in his sleep. Utterly relaxed and sated even though my body was already clamoring for more, I fell asleep quickly.

———

Days passed, and I finished my last show. Back when I had originally scrabbled things together and booked these small shows, I'd envisioned myself traveling alone, and I didn't really know how it would feel. Everything was so different now. Ever since that first fateful night three nights ago, I hadn't been able to stay away from Mack. We carried on the way we had before during the days, being friendly and occasionally chatting in the truck because we'd known each other for years and had that kind of comfort.

At night, we gave up all pretense. We didn't even try to get rooms with two beds anymore. It was only three nights.

Every single night was hotter than the night before—or so it felt—and I kept telling myself we'd burn this madness out of our systems. But no. Every time we came together, the fire burned hotter and hotter. I was *made* of fire and flames the second his mouth claimed mine and his hands began mapping my body.

That morning, I woke wrapped in Mack's strong embrace. Even though I knew this was crazy and reckless and perhaps the stupidest thing I'd ever done when it came to men, I didn't want this to end. It felt too good.

Mack's big palm shifted where it was resting on my belly to slide up and over the curve of my hip. He murmured something unintelligible.

"Mack?" My voice was raspy from sleep.

"Mm-hmm?" he murmured into my hair.

I rolled onto my back and looked toward him. He opened one eye. "Are you awake before me? Are pigs actually flying?"

His lips curled slightly at the corners, and I felt my own tugging into a smile in return. Even before we succumbed to our desires, his preference to hit the road early and my preference to sleep a little later had turned into a joke.

I nudged his abdomen with my elbow, which was like bumping my elbow into a wall. Even at rest, the man was in ridiculously good shape.

"Be serious," I admonished.

He opened his other eye. "I have to be serious?"

I bit my lip and rolled my eyes. "What are we gonna do?"

"I need you to catch me up here. About what?"

I felt my cheeks heating slightly. "Um, this," I said, gesturing back and forth between our naked bodies.

"I know what I'd like to do about this," he murmured.

A teasing, hot look entered his eyes as he lifted his head from the pillow to press a string of hot kisses along my collarbone. My nipples perked up in greeting, and my belly did a little shimmy.

"Mack," I protested.

Of course, then he gave one of my nipples a sweet suck. My body arched reflexively into his touch, and something between a moan and a needy gasp escaped.

I forgot my plan to discuss us. Whether it made sense or was stupid, what mattered was once Mack got his hands and his mouth on my body, he played me like an instrument made just for him.

His mouth teased its way over my belly, the stubble on his cheeks tickling my skin. I went from thinking I needed to set some boundaries to melting like butter in his hands and spreading my knees and practically begging for his touch.

Mack was a very generous lover. His big palms slid up along the insides of my thighs, the calloused surface sending sparks skittering across my skin and causing my hips to rock restlessly. A blunt fingertip circled my clit and teased over my entrance. I was already drenched and slick with arousal.

"Well, good morning, sugar," Mack murmured in that tone of his that held a hint of dirty whenever he spoke when we were skin to skin like this.

His thick fingertip teased around my clit again, and he already had me begging for mercy. "Please, Mack..."

"Whatever you need, sugar."

Two thick fingers sank inside me, knuckle deep. I cried out sharply, thrashing my head on the pillows. His mouth joined the fun with his tongue teasing my clit as he pumped his fingers in and out of me. I heard a muffled curse, and then he was rising over me.

"You make me crazy," he said flatly. "I need inside you. Now."

I looked up to see his strong, hulking form over me. He fisted his long cock in one hand as his shoulder bunched from where the other hand braced him on the bed. When he stroked himself, my mouth actually watered at the sight of pre-cum beading on the tip of his cock and rolling off to drop on my belly.

Just last night, I told him I had an IUD. That was when my hands had been curled on this very headboard, and he fucked me from behind.

"Now, tell me again, just so we're sure. Should I get a condom?" he asked.

He dragged his fingers along the underside of his cock as his eyes held mine and another drop of cum landed on my belly.

I shuddered all over. There was something so raw and sensual about Mack. Everything felt so easy with him. Sex wasn't something that was usually easy for me. I tended to be tense and worried I wasn't getting it right.

I shook my head. "Just fuck me."

"Oh, I love it when you tell me what to do." His lips curled in a sly smile as he held his cock and teased it over my entrance, dragging it up and down and sending sharp jolts of pleasure through me when his cockhead slid over my clit.

Then his crown breached my entrance, and he filled me in a slow slide, the pressure and delicious stretch of him filling me was so intense I almost came right then. He held still for several beats of my heart before lowering his weight over me as his elbows came to rest on either side my head.

"Don't come too fast, Ash. You know I don't like that."

His words were gruff and kind of bossy. I normally didn't enjoy being bossed around, but with Mack, I loved it or rather, my body did. He settled his hips deeper into the cradle of mine, giving a leisurely pump. I let out a ragged moan as a jolt of pleasure sizzled up my spine. I was so slick and tight with him filling me.

Another slow pump with just the right amount of friction over my clit caused me to cry out, my body spasming. "Mack, I don't think I can wait," I gasped as my entire body trembled from the effort of trying to keep from climaxing too fast.

"You're so fucking hot," he muttered. "I can't wait either."

He drew back once more and gave it to me deep and hard. One more time, and I was flying apart, my climax slamming through me and leaving me breathless. I heard his rough shout as one of his hands gripped mine tightly, and then he was shuddering, and I felt the heat of his release filling me.

He rolled instantly, bringing me on top of him where I collapsed in a sated heap on his body. Our breath came in ragged heaves together as we lay like two ships cast ashore after a storm.

After a few minutes, I felt his big hand sifting through my hair. "What did you want to talk about?" he asked.

I lifted my head, resting my chin on my fist on his chest. "We'll be back in Stolen Hearts Valley tomorrow."

"Yeah?"

Chapter Sixteen

MACK

We'll be back in Stolen Hearts Valley tomorrow.

Ash's words echoed in my mind as I stared at her. Fuck me. Ash was so gorgeous, especially right after I'd had my way with her. Her brown hair was messy around her shoulders. Her cheeks were flushed pink, her lips swollen, and her skin dewy.

I'd lost my damn mind a few nights ago, and I kept losing it again and again with her. Ash was like my very own personal drug, and I didn't think I could *ever* get enough of her. I was absolutely addicted to her.

She also happened to be the younger sister of one of my oldest and closest friends. To complicate matters even further, if it was just sex, I could have convinced myself to stop. Sure, I'd get a hard-on every time I laid eyes on her for a little bit, but I was sure I'd get over that eventually. Yet something else was happening here, and it scared the shit out of me while also making the drive to have her as irresistible as anything I'd ever experienced.

"Mack?" Ash prompted.

I slid my fingers through her silky hair down her back to cup her bottom. God, I loved her ass. Loved looking at it, loved touching it, just plain loved it.

"So we are. Are you worried about going home?" I asked, finally addressing her comment. I knew I was dodging a little bit, but I wasn't quite ready to face the meaning that lay behind her question.

"Well, yeah. I think we both have our reasons for avoiding home, but that's not what I'm asking. I think we should establish what our boundaries are going to be. We're not going be traveling together and..."

When her words trailed off, I went ahead and filled in the blanks. "Jackson's one of my best friends, and he might have an opinion about us. Is that what you're after?"

"It's not just Jackson. It's all of our friends. And what the hell are we doing anyway?"

"Having incredible sex," I said, unable to resist the urge to lean up and drag my tongue over the sweet skin of her neck.

Ash trembled slightly, and I felt her pussy squeeze around my cock, which was still inside her.

"You're distracting me," she said, nudging my lips away as if she was pushing a nosy dog out of the way.

"All right, all right. I know," I said. "I don't know what we're doing. I'll be the first to admit I didn't expect this. I've known you forever and never wanted to fuck your brains out until I saw you a few weeks ago. But this is good, really good. Maybe we just play it by ear."

I kind of couldn't believe my train of thought, but I meant it.

Ash stared at me. I knew uncertainty when I saw it, and I knew she didn't know what to think of us. It's just that when we weren't thinking, things were great. Really great.

"Don't start thinking too hard," I warned.

"I don't know how we do that without everybody else knowing what's going on."

"So we don't tell everybody else. We keep it private."

Ash held my gaze with shadows passing through hers. I could hear every resounding beat of my heart as we stared at each other with the thin light of dawn beginning to creep through the curtains. "Okay," she whispered.

Chapter Seventeen

MACK

"Mind passing me the rice?" I asked, catching Dawson's eyes from across the table.

He lifted the large bowl and handed it over. "I bet you missed Dani's cooking," he offered with a grin.

"Course I did. It's been too long since I had a chance to come home."

I spooned the fragrant rice on my plate. After setting the bowl down in the center of the table, I took a bite. "Good lord," I said, not even bothering to hide my moan. "What did you season this with?"

Dani cast me a quick smile as she hurried over from the wide stainless-steel table in the staff kitchen at Stolen Hearts Lodge. She set another bowl down as she replied, "Chipotle and a dash of garlic. It goes really well with the nachos."

"Jesus. I should've moved home sooner," I added after another bite.

My sister, Evie, lifted her blue eyes from across the table. "You should have. We all missed you."

"I'm just glad you're finally here, so Evie can stop worrying about you," Dawson offered as he slid an arm around my sister's shoulders and pressed a kiss to her temple.

Evie understood better than most why I'd been gone, but I knew she missed me. Just as I'd missed her. I was glad she found Dawson this past year. They were a good couple and still so freaking happy it was ridiculous.

"I'm here to stay," I added before spooning a bunch of nachos onto my plate.

"Is Ash coming to dinner?" Shay asked from the other end of the table.

We were eating in the staff kitchen at a fancy version of a picnic table with enough seating for about fifteen people. As usual, I'd taken a seat at the end of one of the bench seats. I knew I was a big guy, and most people didn't appreciate my elbows bumping them constantly. This way, I only had to worry about one side.

My ears perked right up at Shay's question. Jackson happened to come through the swinging door from the hallway at that moment and must've heard Shay's question. "Oh, yeah. Just got her set up in the last empty cabin. She's right beside you," he said, catching my eye as he strode to the table.

Fortunately, my mouth was full of a bite of heavenly nachos so I didn't need to respond. Jackson immediately turned his attention to Shay after I nodded.

Speaking of love, Jackson and Shay were something. I was glad for both of them. They'd had their own lonely journeys through hell and come out on the other side on their own. Jackson, who'd always had a quick wit and joked around, had a rough and somber few years after his time in the military.

Jackson had returned to Stolen Hearts Valley to take over his family's old farm, after his and Ash's father passed away. Their mother had died from cancer two years before that, so there was no one left to deal with the farm except for him and Ash. Their father had turned the farm into a rescue program for animals, so Jackson and Ash built off that by starting the vet clinic and the lodge, which was a high-end outdoor adventure type resort. Ash had left Jackson running the whole thing mostly on his own after her wedding fell apart.

"Guacamole!" Dani called as she hurried over, juggling three bowls in her hands.

Her boyfriend, Wade Ellis, and another old friend snagged two of the bowls and quickly set them down. "Time for you to sit down and eat." Wade patted a spot on the bench beside him. Dani opened her mouth to argue, but Wade caught her hand and shook his head. "We've all got legs. If we need more, we'll get it."

Dani's brown curls swung as she rolled her eyes, but she sat down and accepted a glass of wine that he had poured for her. It seemed all of my friends had paired up in the past few years. Meanwhile, my pulse was revving in anticipation of Ash's presence. I knew I should feel bad. If Jackson had any idea what the last few nights of our trip had comprised, there was no way in hell he'd put her in the cabin right beside mine. I experienced a sharp twinge of guilt.

Yet that twinge was nothing in the face of the roaring current of need I had for Ash. Instead of burning out the embers between us, the fire only burned hotter and faster every time we were together. It was like a brushfire in dry grass that stretched for miles, impossible to put out.

"So how was the trip?" Evie piped up from across the table.

I paused in my chewing and took a gulp of water. "It was good. Glad I ran into Ash. We got to see Niagara Falls, and I've never seen it. Incredible."

Okay, so that wasn't the only reason I was glad I'd run into Ash, but it was still the truth.

"Oh man, you need some of this guacamole on those nachos," Lucas Cole said from beside me.

I took the bowl from him and spooned some on the nachos. I didn't need to be told twice when it came to Dani's food.

"Never been to see the Niagara Falls," Dawson commented, picking up the thread of the conversation.

"It's amazing." Ash's voice came from behind me, and I practically broke my neck from looking over my shoulder so fast.

It felt as if there was an invisible string between Ash and me. Or maybe an electrical wire was a better description. It was exposed and snapping in the open air, sparks flying everywhere.

"Is it?" Evie asked, casting Ash a smile.

"Absolutely. I have to say, it's really hard to describe until you're there," Ash added. Her eyes scanned the table, catching mine briefly where it felt as if there was a little tug between our gazes before she snapped them away. "Guess I'm late. I don't know where to sit."

"Right here," Lucas offered. "I'll make room."

Valentina obligingly moved over with Lucas following suit. Then, Ash was sitting down right beside me. Space was tight, so I could feel the press of her thigh against mine. I shoved a bite of nachos in my mouth. The flavor of the guacamole was enough to drool over, and I was relieved to have the distraction for my senses.

Conversation carried on with many questions lobbed toward Ash and me about our trip. Fortunately, we had plenty of superficial topics to discuss. The food was divine, and it was just plain good to be home with friends.

As the group slowly drifted apart after dinner, I found myself with my hip leaned against the stainless-steel table where Dani worked, chatting with Jackson and Dawson. Of course, half of my attention was snagged on Ash who was still at the table in the back of the room talking with Dani,

Evie, and Shay. This entire tableau was completely normal. In fact, I'd had many an evening just like this while Jackson and Ash were getting the lodge up and running, and I was home on visits. It felt comfortable and easy. An old, almost chilly tension I'd been carrying inside for years eased and warmed a little at the comfort of being here with friends and family who I'd known for almost forever.

The one difference was my acute awareness of Ash and wondering what might happen later tonight when everyone went to bed.

"Yo, Mack," Dawson said.

I glanced in his direction. "Sorry, man, just zoning out. A little tired from the trip."

I wasn't about to say out loud in front of Jackson that I'd heard his sister laugh, and my attention had automatically been drawn in her direction. *Again.*

Dawson nodded but didn't comment further.

"You're on the schedule for the crew starting next week. Will that work?" Jackson asked.

"Of course. You can throw me on starting tomorrow if you want."

Jackson gave me a long look. "Thought you might want a few days to settle in," he commented.

I shrugged. "I like being busy."

Dawson nudged me with his shoulder. "I'm the same way. I hate downtime."

I slid my gaze to him. "Still that bad even though you're shacked up with Evie now?" I teased.

Dawson rolled his eyes. "Hell no. I actually take my days off and spend every hour I can with her. You know how much I love your sister."

I did. Although I hadn't grown up with Dawson, and I didn't know him the way I knew Jackson, it was plain as day he adored Evie. I was happy for them and grinned. "I know you do."

"I'll take a look at the schedule," Jackson said, looping us back on topic. "We're pretty lined out for this week, but there may be a few days to swap out. Do you want to do some work here at the lodge too?"

"You need someone?" I asked in return.

"He always needs someone," Dawson interjected. "I keep telling you, don't expand too fast, man."

"If I have staff I can trust, it's not as big of a deal. Seriously, I could use you," Jackson said, his gaze sobering as he held mine. "I want to expand the rescue program. We've got the room, and the need is constant. With Ash home now, she can pick up some of the slack at the vet clinic, and we can get going on some more building. We need to build another barn with a kennel and space for the misfits."

"The misfits?" I returned.

"Just what I was wondering," Dawson chimed in.

"Rescues that aren't too common. We usually get dogs, cats and horses. We don't get very many pigs, or goats, or opossums," Jackson explained.

Walker, a guy I'd only met today but who'd been working here for the past year or so, paused beside us. "Everett is the best mascot your vet clinic ever had."

"Who's Everett?" I asked.

Jackson flashed a smile. "Everett's an opossum Jade found on the side of the road a few months ago. Jade would've killed me if we hadn't kept him."

Walker grinned. "It's not like you would've said no. Anyway, I'm outta here. Catch y'all tomorrow."

"Tell Jade I said hey," Ash called as Walker strode past the table on his way to the door in the back.

He waved over his shoulder. "Will do," he called in return.

"Okay," I said, looping back to our conversation. "You need space. Dude, I'm in. You know I love to build, and I'll work with you any day."

Jackson clapped me on the shoulder. "Perfect. How

about we leave the crew schedule as is, and you come by tomorrow and meet me at my office in the clinic? We can start drawing up those plans. You're better at that shit than I am."

Chapter Eighteen

ASH

Resting my hands on my hips, I spun in a slow circle and looked around my new home. Jackson had been busy in the year and a half I'd been gone from Stolen Hearts Valley. Among other things he'd worked on, he'd added a number of newer guest cabins, some of which were for staff.

This one was adorable. The gable roof allowed a vaulted ceiling, and the space felt large and spacious. I could see the moonlight gilding the mountain range across the valley and shimmering through the windows that ran floor to ceiling on one side. Wide plank hardwood flooring with a light finish and walls painted a soft cream gave the room a bright, airy feeling.

A low dresser sat against the wall opposite the foot of the bed. There was a small round table with chairs over in the efficiency kitchen in the corner. All of the furnishings were wood with clean, modern lines.

I hadn't even walked around the space earlier when Shay and Jackson brought me over. They brought me here after a minor standoff about me staying in the farmhouse with them. I'd pointed out that space was theirs, and I preferred to have some privacy. Both of those things were true. That would've been my request even if I weren't wondering whether Mack was going to come over tonight.

Striding across the room, I stepped into the bathroom. "Ooh," I said aloud even though no one was here to hear me.

It was tiled in soft blue with a large oval bathtub in one corner. Peering inside the shower in the other corner, I saw a rainfall showerhead in the center of the ceiling with shower jets along the walls. That will be perfect after a long day out hiking, or climbing, or in my case, working at the vet clinic.

I pushed open a small door to discover a closet with shelving. Jackson had gone all out to make the spaces really nice. Our old guest cabins were also pretty new, but these were definitely a level up.

Returning to the main room, I opened the refrigerator to discover Shay must have stocked it for me. There were gourmet cheese and fresh sandwich meats, along with some bread and fruit. I smiled when I saw the bag of coffee from Wake & Bake Café, one of my favorite places in downtown Stolen Hearts Valley. Sliding my phone out of my pocket, I sent her a quick text to thank her. Before I even got the phone back in my pocket, she replied with a smiley face emoticon.

I set my phone on the kitchen table and walked to the door to slide off my shoes. Carrying my bag into the closet off the bathroom, I began unpacking. I didn't have much since I'd been living on the road for the past year and a half. I had some things in storage in the farmhouse, but I'd pared down before I left.

Just as I was folding my T-shirts and putting them on the shelves, I heard a knock on my door. I was almost embarrassed at how my pulse leaped. It lunged erratically and then sped off as if trying to win a race against an invisible competitor.

Anticipation hummed in my veins as I trotted across the floor like a happy little pony. Even as I reminded myself sternly it could be somebody else, I wanted it to be Mack. I *really* wanted it to be Mack.

Look at you, already falling for him like an idiot. Don't be stupid again.

My critical voice was always quick with the comments, and I mentally sighed. Maybe if I'd listened to it before, I would've caught on much earlier to the fact that my ex-fiancé was screwing around with someone. I also probably would've had more sense about deciding to try a stupid friends-with-benefits thing just because some guy was charming and sexy. I genuinely hadn't fallen for Kyle. But my arrangement with him, for lack of a better description, had done a number on my self-esteem.

There was another knock just as I reached the door. Curling my hand around the doorknob, I took a breath before I opened it. My heart kicked excitedly against my ribs when I found Mack standing there.

His hand was curled on the top of the doorframe with his elbow resting against the side. He was all relaxed, sexy swagger, and I wanted to eat him up.

"Hey," he said, his gruff voice sending a prickle down my spine.

I just stood there, smiling like a fool until his slow grin stretched from one corner of his mouth to the other. "Am I allowed to come in?"

Biting my lip, I peered around his side. "Is anyone around?" I whispered.

"No, ma'am," he said somberly. "Our cabins are the last ones on the path."

He didn't wait for me to say any more and dropped his hand from above, resting both hands on my hips as he walked me backward into the cabin. He kicked the door shut lightly with his boot.

For several beats of my heart, we just stared at each other. The air shimmered to life around us—hot and electric. Mack's hands were still resting on my hips when he took a step closer.

He was a potent force. Whenever he was close and towering over me, I could feel his presence surrounding me. I felt protected by him and also stripped bare of my defenses.

His hands slid up my sides, one resting just to the side of my breast where his thumb moved back and forth in an idle path, and the other lifting to cup my nape. My pulse skittered under the feel of his thumb resting along the side of my neck.

That was how bad I had it for Mack. With just a tiny touch—the pad of his thumb resting on my skin—I was practically putty in his hands. Heat shot through me, and my breath came in shallow pants.

"How was your day?" he asked as his gaze locked with mine.

That was something I hadn't experienced before Mack. When he turned his attention on me, his focus was absolute. The intensity elicited restlessness inside me, and I almost wanted to shy away. At the same time, I was ensnared and savored the attention.

I swallowed. "Good."

We had arrived in Stolen Hearts Valley late this morning. We'd been immediately drawn into lunch where I fielded questions about my arm, and we filled everyone in on the accident. After that, Shay and Jackson took me to the farmhouse, and I got updates on the lodge, the vet clinic, and the rescue program. I didn't even know where Mack had gone during those hours. I hadn't seen him again until dinner.

"How was yours?" I managed to add, my voice coming out husky.

"Good. Are you gonna kick me out tonight?"

My pulse leaped wildly with his question, practically answering for me. His hand slid around to cup my cheek, his thumb sliding across my bottom lip in a sensual pass. Mack was magic with his hands. It didn't matter what he did; he turned me on like crazy.

I shook my head slowly. "No, but we need a plan for tomorrow morning."

"Oh, I have a plan for morning," he replied.

Not a single word of what he said was inappropriate, yet the look in his eyes was so *dirty*. My pussy clenched, and I felt my slick arousal. I wanted him to bend me over and fuck me. Right now.

As if he could actually read my mind, he added, "That bed is perfect."

"Perfect for what?"

His tongue slid across his teeth. "The height. Turn around. Well, after you get out of those jeans."

I was *that* easy when it came to Mack because I didn't even hesitate. I loved being bossed around by him. Because whenever he did, the result was me usually experiencing more than one climax and falling asleep fabulously sated.

Sometime later, after testing out the height of the bed and the amazing shower and then collapsing in a heap following round two, I spoke into Mack's chest where my cheek was resting. "Morning. We need a morning plan."

Mack's hand was resting on my back. He slid it down my spine to palm my ass and give it a squeeze. "Told you. I already have morning plans."

"What are they?"

"You."

I lifted my head and found him waggling his eyebrows with a grin. "I'm serious. When the sun's up, people will notice if you're leaving. Plus, Dani gets up at five. Or maybe even earlier for all I know."

Mack's gaze sobered, and he lifted a hand to brush my mussed hair away from my face. I couldn't decide if I was more disappointed that he wasn't squeezing my bottom, or if the clench of my heart at his easy gentleness was better. As much as I savored it, his gentleness just might be my undoing.

"I know, sugar. I'm up early whether I want to be or not. I'll be out of here, and I promise Dani won't notice." He was quiet as he looked at me. "I know I said we could keep this between us, but I'm not a fan of secrets."

"And I'm not a fan of gossip. Not that I think Jackson should have a say in my sex life, but he'll probably have an opinion if he knows what's going on."

"I know. Maybe we just tell him."

Chapter Nineteen

MACK

"It's none of Jackson's business. I don't want him to get all overprotective. Plus, it's not worth the trouble of our friends wondering what's going on when we don't even know what we're doing. It's just really great sex. I'm sure it'll burn itself out. Right?"

Ash's words had played on a loop in my brain for the past few days. I might not have memorized them exactly, but it was damn close to what she said after I suggested we not keep *us* a secret. She'd punctuated them with a wide-eyed look and a quick shake of her head. Anxiety had flashed across her face and flickered deep in her eyes.

My girl was guarded. Except when we were naked and in the throes of passion. Otherwise, I thought I understood just how thoroughly Ash guarded her heart because it was something I understood deeply myself. For entirely different reasons, I'd always figured I'd never fall in love.

I never wanted anyone to matter so much that I had to deal with the pain of loss. Even worse, feeling helpless to keep someone I loved safe. I still had my other sister, Evie, Krista's twin, to worry about. I knew Evie felt the loss of Krista probably even more sharply than I did. I wasn't a twin myself, but I'd been witness to their bond together when we were growing up.

I loved my parents, but they weren't great. Not even close. As a result of their emotionally neglectful and harsh parenting, us kids had bonded tightly. I'd been Evie and Krista's older brother, the one who was supposed to keep them safe, but I'd completely failed Krista.

So yeah, I understood the need to make sure no one got too close. Because if no one ever mattered enough, then you didn't have to worry about losing anyone. Not ever again.

Yet here I was with my girl in my thoughts. For as long as I could remember, Ash had been a friend, and I'd never wanted her. This attraction to her was like a bolt of lightning out of a sunny sky. It was that startling.

Perhaps that was what made it all the more powerful. It was so potent it had wrapped around my heart and wasn't letting go.

"There you are," Jackson said as he came walking into his office at the vet clinic where Shay had parked me a few minutes ago. His presence kicked my thoughts off the tracks of Ash.

Jackson shared Ash's brown hair although his was short and on the shaggy side. He sat down at the round table in his office across from me and leaned back in the chair with a sigh. "Sorry I'm running behind, man. Had an emergency surgery this morning."

"No worries," I replied. "I took a look at the stuff you emailed over last night. Thought I'd ask a few questions, and then I'll get some designs started. Unless it's complicated, I can probably have some options for you to review in a few days."

"That'd be awesome," Jackson said, his eyes crinkling at the corners with his smile.

Looking into Jackson's blue eyes, I immediately thought of Ash. I felt a twinge of guilt and kicked it aside. I couldn't be obsessing about her, not while I was with him.

"Y'all need some coffee?" Shay asked when she stopped in the doorway and held a coffee pot aloft.

The moment Jackson looked at Shay, his entire expression softened. "Always."

She stepped into the room, pausing beside a small table just inside the door and curling her index finger around two coffee mugs. Her blond ponytail swung as she turned back.

"How are you liking it here?" I asked as she filled a coffee cup and slid it in front of me.

"I love it."

Jackson slid his arm around her waist and gave her a squeeze at the hips while she filled his coffee cup. "She's basically running everything except the kitchen and the restaurant. That's Dani's domain."

"And it's best we keep it that way." She leaned over and dropped a kiss on Jackson's cheek. "I have enough between the vet clinic and the rescue program. I didn't know you could do building design, Mack. I'm so excited you're going to be in charge of the new barn for the rescue program," she added when she looked over at me.

I took a swallow of my coffee. "Damn, this is good. Thank you. And I'm glad to help. Can't believe I walked into the crew job and this."

"Well, everyone's glad you're home. Evie's overjoyed," Shay commented.

"I know she is. It's good to be back home."

At that moment, I heard Ash's voice talking to someone. "He looks great. Our tech will help with a nail trim, and then just bring him in next month so I can check his levels," Ash was saying.

I presumed she was talking about someone's pet. Her voice faded, and I was relieved to be able to bring my attention back to Jackson and Shay. The phone rang, and Shay spun away. "Y'all have a good meeting. I'm gonna grab that call."

After she hurried off, I looked over at Jackson. "Y'all seem to be doing good," I observed.

He finished a swallow of coffee and nodded. "We are. Kind of surprises me still."

"I'm glad. All right, tell me how much space you're looking for, where you want to put it, and then I'll see what I can draw up for you."

Jackson started explaining, and we were deep into discussing the options when an opossum came wandering into the room.

"Is this Everett?" I asked with a grin.

Jackson nodded and chuckled as the opossum came right up to him and rested his paws on Jackson's knees. "Oh, yeah. Jade found him after he got hit by a car. He was banged up, but he survived. We tried to rehab him well enough to release him back into the wild, but the injury on his back hips was too severe. No way he could move quick enough to survive in the wild, so we kept him since we can."

Jackson reached for a treat in a bowl in the center of the table and tossed me one. "Just call his name. He'll be your best friend in about a minute."

Treat in hand, I called, "Everett."

The opossum looked across the table at me and then disappeared from view before popping up right between my knees. I laughed while he held the treat between his small paws.

At the sound of footsteps, I glanced up to see Ash appear in the doorway. She smiled at Jackson before her eyes shifted to me. "Isn't he cute?"

"Adorable."

I wanted to kiss her, but that wasn't an option. I wanted Ash, and now I wanted more than what we'd had so far. When her eyes locked on mine, it felt as though a string pulled tight between us, and my heart started to kick up a racket in my chest.

"Ash?" Jackson's voice nudged into my awareness.

Ash snapped her eyes from mine. "Yeah?"

"I was asking how the schedule's working out," Jackson said.

"Great. Shay's got it so organized; it's nice."

"You didn't need to jump right in. I could've covered all the appointments today."

Everett patted my knee with a paw, so I lifted him onto my lap and let myself absorb the sight of Ash. With Jackson facing her, I didn't have to worry about him noticing. Her hair was pulled up into a bun on top of her head with a pen stuck through it. She wore jeans with her tennis shoes and a white lab coat over everything.

She was sexy as hell, and I couldn't wait until tonight.

I caught up to the conversation when Ash said, "I'll cover every day. With Mack here, y'all can do some planning for that rescue building. I'm all about helping with the planning, but I know nothing about building." Her eyes finally flicked in my direction again.

"Ash, you don't have to work your tail off right away. Why don't you take some downtime and catch up with everybody?" Jackson commented.

Ash wrinkled her nose. "I've missed being in the clinic. Let me just get back in the swing of things."

Jackson shrugged. "Whatever you want."

With a wave, Ash hurried away. Jackson ran a hand through his hair as he looked back in my direction. "Ash doesn't appreciate when I have an opinion about anything. I can't even tell her to take a break."

"No need to worry about it. Just let her settle in at her own pace," I offered noncommittally.

"How was she doing when you ran into her? I never did like that Kyle guy."

I shifted my shoulders. "All right, I guess. She got a little cranky with me, but once we settled into a groove, it was fine. She says she's moving home for good."

Jackson nodded slowly. "How about you?"

Jackson was easygoing, but he knew why I'd been scarce the past few years. I took a slow swallow of my coffee, tracing my thumb along the curve of the handle as I lowered the mug to the table. Holding Jackson's gaze, I nodded. "Yeah. I'm home for good."

He was quiet, and then a slow smile broke out across his face. "Damn glad to have you home. Now, let's get into the details."

Jackson and I settled into a few hours of planning for the new building he wanted. We worked until Wade poked his head in the doorway. "Y'all want to meet at Lost Deer Bar in about an hour?"

"Are we having dinner in the staff kitchen first?" Jackson returned.

Wade shook his head. "Nah. I'm rounding everybody up. Dani's not feeling good."

"We'll see you there then," I replied.

Chapter Twenty

ASH

"I'm sorry, what?" I asked.

Shay burst out laughing. "Crazy, right? I would've died of embarrassment."

"She did faint," Evie added dryly.

"I don't know if I could get over it if I met a guy that way," I offered.

Valentina, whose cheeks were almost as red as her hair, let out a little laugh.

"As you can see, they got over the vibrator incident," Shay offered.

"Seriously now. You ordered a vibrator in the mail, and Lucas opened it by accident? You're not making this up?" I queried.

Valentina's curls bounced on her shoulders as she shook her head. "Definitely not making it up."

"I don't think Valentina knows how to lie," Evie chimed in.

Although Valentina had been working at the lodge and handling all of the bookkeeping and accounting, I didn't know her too well. Dani had hired her after I'd started traveling. Now that I'd had a chance to spend some time with her, I liked her. She had a refreshing openness to her.

"I'm happy for Lucas. He's always been such a nice guy," I said.

"I know, and he's ridiculously in love with Valentina," Evie added.

"No more so than Dawson's in love with you," I offered. "Seems like everybody fell in love while I was gone."

Shay swung her arm around my shoulders and squeezed. "You'll find the right guy. I never thought I would."

I looked into her warm eyes and smiled. "I'm so glad you moved here. You deserve the best, and Jackson's perfect for you."

They'd married just this spring, and I'd made it home for a weekend for the wedding. We didn't comment on it because there was no need, but Shay had been through hell with her violent and abusive ex. I'd worried I would lose her completely as she slowly pulled away from all of her friendships, but after a particularly brutal assault by her ex, Shay had called me. I'd insisted she come and stay at the farm even though I'd known I was planning to leave for a while.

That move set the wheels in motion for her and Jackson to fall in love just as I always thought they should.

"That's nice you're so happy for me, but my point is you can find someone too," Shay added.

I shrugged. "Maybe or maybe not. I don't have the best luck with men."

"Neither did I," Shay said with a nudge of her elbow in my side.

"Where is Dani?" I suddenly asked. I'd been expecting her to show any minute.

"She wasn't feeling good. I think she's coming down with a cold," Evie offered. "Wade told all of us we needed to come out here for dinner. Apparently, the guys are meeting us here."

My heartbeat kicked up, and I wondered if the guys

included Mack. Ever since I'd seen him this afternoon in Jackson's office, I'd been impatient for tonight when darkness fell and I could see him. Considering that I'd spent almost twenty-four hours a day with him for the past several weeks, I missed him.

Which was ridiculous. The waitress stopped to take our dinner orders, and while she was circling the table, the guys arrived. Lucas, Dawson, and Jackson arrived first. I honestly, really truly, wasn't envious of my friends' happiness in their respective relationships. Yet there was a twinge in my heart, a little pinch of loneliness.

Then a voice in my thoughts, so consistent, chimed in to remind me that maybe I'd never get lucky in love. That was why I'd sworn off looking for romance. My self-esteem was battered enough as it was.

I tried to ignore the shaft of disappointment at Mack's absence. There was some shuffling in the chairs around the table.

"Anyone else coming?" I asked as I looked around the table and realized I was the only single person present.

Jackson leaned his elbows on the table and looked around Shay to me. "Wade and Mack are coming, but I'm not sure how far behind us they are."

"Did y'all actually carpool here?" I asked in return.

"Yes, ma'am," Dawson drawled. "I'm all about saving the environment."

Evie rolled her eyes. "There's no high occupancy vehicle lane on the highways in the mountains here," she teased.

"Yeah, but I'm hitching a ride home with Valentina," Lucas interjected.

Valentina lifted her eyes to him. I happened to be looking in their direction, and the intense look that passed between them for nothing more than a few seconds nearly took my breath away. God, I wanted a man to look at me the way Lucas looked at Valentina—as if she was the very center of his universe.

Tearing my eyes away, I reminded myself that those kinds of looks were the reason I hadn't wanted to bunk in the farmhouse where Jackson and Shay lived. I knew I could, and I knew there was plenty of space, but I didn't need a daily reminder of what I didn't have. I excused myself to go to the bathroom.

Moments later, I splashed water on my face and dabbed it dry with a paper towel. Staring in the mirror, I surveyed my chestnut brown hair. I didn't have honey gold locks like Shay, or wild red curls like Valentina, or the dark glossy hair Evie had. She shared that with Mack, except his was short. My hair was just plain brown. My breath came out with a sigh as I steeled myself to deal with being surrounded by all of my friends who were deeply in love.

Stepping into the hallway, I widened my eyes when I found Mack leaning against the wall opposite the door into the women's restroom. My hand flew to my chest, and my pulse rioted.

"Hey," he said, biting the corner of his lip.

"Hey." That word came out just barely above a whisper. Mack had that effect, making me feel like a foolish schoolgirl with a crush.

"Excuse me," a woman said.

"Oh, sorry!" I jumped out of the way, realizing I was blocking the bathroom door completely.

She pushed past me, and the door clicked shut behind her. Mack's arm snaked out, his index finger curling into the belt loop on my jeans as he tugged me closer.

"What are you doing?" I hissed.

"Saying hello," he murmured right before his hand slid into my hair, and he drew me close for a quick, plundering kiss. It couldn't have been more than three or four seconds, but his tongue swept into my mouth, and he pulled back with a light nip on my bottom lip. I was flushed all over and breathless for more.

Staring at him, I took a step back and tried to catch my breath. "Anyone could have seen that," I whispered.

"Nobody did." His knowing eyes held mine, and my heart flipped in my chest. "Go back to the table," he said softly. "I'll be there in a minute."

I opened my mouth to argue, but the bathroom door bumped me from behind. The woman didn't even look in our direction as she hurried back toward the bar. Right then, the screen door at the back of the hallway opened, and a group of people came through. With a frustrated huff, I turned and walked back into the restaurant. My lips were tingling. I hated to admit that I enjoyed that kiss, but I did. I didn't simply enjoy it; I *loved* it.

Some arguments were worth having with myself, but I was mostly resigned to the reality that my attraction to Mack ran so deep it felt like a bottomless well. I just needed to figure out how the hell to deal with it. I returned to the table to listen to an argument about next year's college basketball season. "I know I'm home when we're arguing about basketball."

Dawson looked my way, his eyes crinkling at the corners with a teasing smile. "Of course. We're just debating UNC's chances."

"Are they any good this year?"

"They're always good," Jackson murmured. "You need to get back in the swing of things. You did graduate from UNC."

"You know I'm a Heels fan. It's just I've been gone a while and not many places are this insane about college basketball," I replied when Mack arrived at the table. Only then did I realize the only chair left was the one right beside me, opposite from where Shay was sitting.

Mack slipped into it, commenting, "True story. North Carolina is where people go crazy when it comes to basketball."

Our waitress arrived to take orders from the guys.

"Thank God," Mack murmured under his breath while Dawson was ordering. "I'm starving."

Sliding my gaze to his, I asked, "Long day?"

He nodded. "Oh, yeah. Did a workout this morning on the climbing wall out at the station and then holed up with Jackson in the office for hours discussing the plans for the new barn."

My heart flipped again, and I felt so exposed. Being with Mack like this with our friends almost hurt a little. Because I liked him. So very much.

"Why are we making it a barn, by the way?" I asked, looking toward my brother and relieved for the distraction of any topic of conversation.

"Because it'll match everything," Jackson said.

"I asked the same thing," Mack said under his breath at my shoulder.

I resisted the urge to giggle and tried to ignore the shiver skating over my skin at the sound of his low, gruff whisper.

Keeping my focus on my brother—my freaking brother —I replied, "It makes sense, but we need to make use of the space upstairs."

"We will. Mack already has a plan, don't you?" Jackson countered, nudging his chin in Mack's direction.

Jackson blessedly looked away when the waitress reached his side. With the noise in the bar and everyone around us talking, no one paid much attention to Mack and me. He winked and slid his giant palm on my thigh. I knocked it off and happily took my water from the waitress and the appetizer of chipotle-seasoned sweet potato fries.

When I set the plate down, Mack commented immediately, "Please tell me you're going to share."

I was about to deny him until I saw his eyes and heard his stomach growl. With a sigh, I pushed the plate between us. "You look like a starving puppy. I can't say no."

Mack took a fry, closing his eyes and letting out a moan when he put it in his mouth. "Oh my God, these are so fucking good," he said, not even caring that he was talking while he was chewing.

Evie commented, "Geez, Mack, you didn't learn any better table manners while you were gone, did you?"

Mack popped another sweet potato fry in his mouth and waggled his eyebrows as he shook his head. "Damn," he added after he finished chewing, "I forgot how good the food was here."

The waitress made her way to him and took his order. After that, the next few hours were a unique form of torture. I had Mack right at my side. He kept his hands to himself with the exception of his strong, muscled thigh pressing against mine. Because he was teasing me, he'd pulled his chair almost flush with mine when he sat down.

It was good to be home, better than I'd even let myself hope for. I loved my friends, and I loved my home. It was only when everybody was getting up to leave that I realized I needed to figure out how I was getting home.

"Do you need a ride?" Shay asked, glancing in my direction. Jackson had his arm around her waist, and I figured if I rode with them, I'd be squished in the extra cab of Jackson's truck while they canoodled on the way home.

"I'll ride with Mack," I said before even letting myself think about it. "Y'all are parking over by the farmhouse, and he'll be over by the lodge, which is closer to my place."

If it weren't for the fact that Mack and I had been naked together for too many nights already, I probably wouldn't feel my cheeks getting hot. Fortunately, the lighting at the bar was low. Shay simply shrugged and gave a wave over her shoulder as she and Jackson walked ahead of us out the bar.

Mack stayed a comfortable distance behind me, but it didn't matter. I was hyper-aware of his presence, and every hair on my body vibrated. I felt my skin prickling at knowing he was nearby. When we approached the door to the women's restroom, I glanced over my shoulder. "I'm gonna take a quick bathroom break. Do you mind?"

Mack shook his head. "Course not. I'll wait."

Somehow, his benign words felt loaded. It didn't escape my notice that every person we'd been here with was already gone with the door to the parking lot swinging shut behind Jackson only seconds earlier. I didn't know if Mack was going to wait in the hallway or out in the parking lot, but I needed a few seconds to gather myself. For the second time tonight, I splashed cold water on my face and dabbed it dry. The stiff paper towel didn't feel great on my skin, but desperate times and all that. I was flushed all over, and I could feel the slick arousal between my thighs.

I was having stupid thoughts tonight, thoughts where I wished maybe I wasn't such a bad bet when it came to romance. Oh, I knew Mack and I had chemistry, enough to burn down buildings, but I was pretty sure he didn't want a relationship, and I wasn't so sure I could handle one. My past choices in men had left my self-esteem pretty shredded.

Taking a deep breath, I told myself I could handle this. When I opened the bathroom door, it felt like a replay of the moment earlier tonight. Mack was leaning against the wall. He lifted his head when I stepped out. Quick and smooth, he reached across the hallway and hooked his finger in my belt loop again. In a breath, I was standing right in front of him, my nipples puckering in sheer happiness and my heart doing a little shimmy in my chest.

"What are you doing?" I whispered, instantly annoyed with myself that I was repeating my very question from earlier tonight.

"Everyone's gone, sugar. Sitting beside you all night, I behaved and kept my hands to myself."

His words were so earnest that I laughed softly, dropping my forehead against his chest and taking a breath. When I lifted my head, his lips were on mine, claiming my mouth with such raw confidence that my knees melted, and I practically sagged against him. Of course, collapsing against Mack was all kinds of awesome. He felt so good and strong and muscly. When he drew back, I was breathless, and blood was rushing through my ears with every thundering beat of my heart.

We stared at each other, and I was gratified to feel Mack's heartbeat thudding rapidly against my breasts, and his breath coming in short rapid bursts.

"What are we doing, Mack?" I whispered

"I'm taking you home, sugar."

"But..."

Mack put his finger over my lips. "Do you want me?" he asked

I rolled my eyes. "Obviously. I'm ridiculously easy with you."

His eyes crinkled at the corners with a smile as he regarded me. "Good thing. Because I want you so fucking bad, and I don't really care if it's complicated. Now, come on. Let me take you home, and then you can convince me we still need to keep this a secret."

Chapter Twenty-One

MACK

By some miracle, I didn't fuck Ash in my truck. I seriously considered it, but there were too many unknown variables. Anywhere we parked along the way home could mean someone we knew driving by. Doing the dirty deed in the truck at the lodge parking lot was a surefire "no" from Ash.

I satisfied the fiery need to touch her by unbuttoning her jeans and sliding my fingers in her panties just so I could make sure she was wet. As if there was any doubt.

"What are you doing?" she whispered for the third time tonight.

"Just wondering if you're as bad off as me," I drawled as I put my truck in park behind the main building at the lodge. "Don't worry. Nobody can see my hands in your pants but you and me."

She bit her lip and cast me something along the lines of a glare when I withdrew my hand. She buttoned her jeans, looking over as I sucked her arousal off my fingers. The heat that flared in her eyes was almost as good as she tasted.

As we walked into the trees, I felt Ash turn quickly at a

rustling sound. She looked down and then laughed as we saw Gloria, the lodge's resident friendly pig, meandering out behind the kitchen at the back of the restaurant. Her curly tail was illuminated from the lights behind the lodge.

Ash glanced over her shoulder at me. "I'm guessing she's headed to the rescue barn."

"Kinda late," I observed.

"Sometimes she goes looking for the scraps from the restaurant," Ash commented, her voice low in the darkness.

I reached for Ash's hand. For a second, I thought she was going to swat me away, but she didn't. Her hand relaxed, and she laced her fingers through mine. The pine needles crunched under our feet as we walked. The way the lodge was set up, the two main barns had been renovated into housing for the guests with the restaurant and staff kitchen in one of them. There were cabins for staff who lived at the lodge, and additional guest cabins were scattered across the property. The ones for staff were mostly clustered toward the restaurant, and solar-powered lights mounted along the ground kept the path lit.

Ash stiffened for a moment when we heard someone's voice through the trees, but she didn't release my hand. She stopped in the path just before we reached the last two cabins, the first of which was mine with hers just beyond that.

She peered up at me. "Well?"

"Well, what?"

Although I couldn't see her face clearly because there wasn't much light where we stood, I imagined her cheeks tinged pink. She lifted a shoulder in a small shrug. "I don't know. Where are you staying?"

I was feeling bold, galvanized somehow by knowing she wanted to keep us a secret. I also knew she was forbidden. Not completely. But at the moment, Jackson knew nothing. Until she let me tell him, we were a secret, and I knew she wanted it to stay that way.

Turning to face her, I lifted a hand and caught a lock of her hair, letting it slide like silk through my fingers. "Are you asking if I intend to do what I've been doing every night? Because, sugar, I want to fuck you until you forget all the rules you're making about why we shouldn't be together."

Ash's breath hitched, and her eyes widened as she stared at me. Without another word, I dropped my hand from her hair and turned, striding quickly toward her cabin. We hadn't discussed it, but that was where we had spent every night. Truthfully, I hadn't even tried to make my cabin feel like a home yet.

We stepped through the door quickly. Somewhere between standing in the trees outside and kicking the door shut, Ash became as frantic as me. She spun around and shoved my back against the door.

"You're pushing it," she murmured when she nipped lightly at my neck.

I chuckled even though I ached all over for her, drawn so tight inside I knew the fierce need wouldn't abate until I found my release.

"Am I?" I murmured as she yanked at the buttons on my fly and slid her hand in my boxers to curl her palm around my swollen shaft.

She wasn't waiting. I already knew once Ash made up her mind, she threw herself into the moment. In a matter of seconds, my hand was gripping her hair as she swirled her tongue around my cock before dragging it along the under-side and gripping me at the base. My head thumped loudly against the door behind me.

Ash let out a throaty, sexy as hell laugh. I could feel the vibration of it around my cock when she took me in her warm, slick mouth. She knew how to make me beg for mercy. In no time, she had me on the edge of release, but I didn't want to let go until I was one with her.

"Ash," I bit out through gritted teeth.

"Mm-hmm?" She drew away with a swirl of her tongue around the tip of my cock.

"I need to be inside you."

Our clothes came off in a rush, tossed messily on the floor. Then I was stretching out on the bed and lifting one of her knees to hook in my elbow. I positioned my cock at her entrance and stroked in fully. My forehead fell to hers as we breathed together. I could feel her channel already rippling around me. My heartbeat thundered through my body, and heat sizzled at the base of my spine.

"I love being inside you," I murmured.

Ash let out a low cry as I pulled back slightly and gave a slow pump of my hips into her. My release was hovering right on the edge, but I needed Ash with me. After another pump, I felt her tremble and clench around me.

The relief of my release was intense, whipsawing through me like hot electricity. I poured into her with every shudder as I distantly heard my name.

I loved it when Ash cried my name.

———

Closing my eyes, I savored the rich flavor of coffee as I swallowed it. Setting my coffee mug down on the table, I opened my eyes and looked over at Ash where she stood by the counter in the small kitchen area. "Coffee's amazing. Thank you."

She smiled over at me. "Bagel with cream cheese coming right up."

Just then, there was a knock on the cabin door. Ash's eyes went comically wide, and her hand froze where it was curled on the handle of the toaster oven. "Who is it?" she whispered loudly.

"Don't stress. We're both dressed, and my cabin is right next door. We'll just say I came over for coffee and breakfast."

Ash's hand dropped from the toaster, and she nodded before hurrying over to the door. Glancing over, I could see the tension in her shoulders and figured she was probably going to give me hell for lingering here this morning.

Maybe I wasn't worthy of it, but I liked Ash. Maybe I more than liked her. I wanted to just tell Jackson about us when Ash stopped freaking out about it. I was prepared for him to want to kick my ass, but I could take my lumps.

When she swung the door open, I could see Shay on the small porch. "Hey. I was wondering if you wanted to come do the feeding rounds with me this morning. You told me to stop by," Shay said.

The entire cabin, with the exception of the bathroom, was visible from the doorway, so I lifted a hand in a wave. "Morning, Shay," I called. "I stopped by for coffee and a bagel."

She smiled. "Come on in," Ash finally said.

Although it was still early, not even six a.m., the humidity carried inside with the door open only briefly. It was summer in the Blue Ridge Mountains, and that meant hot days and only slightly cooler nights.

The door clicked shut as Shay stepped in, giving a cursory glance around the space. "Oh, you already made it kind of cute," she said, her eyes landing on the curtains Ash had somehow managed to procure this week.

Ash was walking behind Shay, and mouthed, "Behave." Following that, she added, "Want some coffee, Shay?"

I was planning to behave, if only because I didn't want Ash to kick my ass just yet.

"I'll never say no to coffee," Shay replied when she stopped beside the table.

"Coming right up. Have a seat," Ash said as she walked to the counter.

Shay sat down beside me. In another moment, Ash handed her a cup of coffee and then brought my bagel over before looking toward Shay again. "Bagel?"

"No thanks. I'll start with coffee. After we finish with the feeding, I'll grab breakfast at the lodge."

"Mind waiting a few minutes while I have one?" Ash returned.

"Absolutely not. I need time to enjoy my coffee anyway."

Shay glanced at us as I took a bite of my bagel. "So it sounds like y'all had a good trip. How's your arm?" She gestured toward Ash's forearm.

Ash looked down at her arm. "Much better." She was wearing a lightweight blouse over a tank top, so she rolled her sleeve up. "I'm not even wearing a bandage now."

The skin was still pink, but it had healed over. Every time I thought about that moment, my heart twisted uncomfortably in my chest.

"God, this is good coffee. No wonder you came over for it," Shay said, flashing a grin in my direction.

I nodded. "Exactly. I have no problem taking advantage of Ash's superior coffee skills."

Shay glanced around again, her eyes landing on Ash's guitar, tucked away in its case. "You planning to play anywhere soon?" she asked, looking toward Ash.

Ash nodded. "Of course. Now that I'm back, I need to make a few calls. I can always play at Lost Deer on open mic nights, and I can get paid for small shows at some places in Asheville."

Shay nodded. "Good. Let me know when because you know I'll be there." She paused to sip her coffee. "I hear from Jackson that y'all pretty much hammered out the building plans, right?"

I sure hoped she was oblivious to Ash's tension because it was glaringly obvious to me. Ash kept throwing me nervous glances and drumming her fingertips on the table after she sat down.

"Oh yeah, we're ready to roll. I'm gonna make some calls to line up some of the subcontractors for the dirt work and foundation, but once that's done, everybody here can handle the rest."

"It's gonna be awesome. We really need more space," Shay commented.

"I can't thank you enough for stepping in and helping so much with the rescue program," Ash said.

Shay smiled. "I love it. Plus, don't go thinking you're gonna take over now that you're home. You're going to be plenty busy with the vet clinic. But this way, you and I can take turns with the feedings and cover for each other. I know you could figure it out without me, but I can tell you all the current quirks."

Ash grinned. "I saw Gloria last night. I'm guessing somebody gave her some restaurant leftovers."

Shay rolled her eyes. "That pig is so spoiled, but the lodge wouldn't be what it is without her and Squeaky," she said, referencing a mini pig who was often Gloria's shadow. Though Squeaky didn't wander quite as much as Gloria did.

They chatted casually about business things while I finished my bagel and Ash ate half of hers. Shay's phone vibrated, and she tugged it out of her pocket.

"How about you meet me up at the rescue barn? We've got a payment issue at the reception desk at the clinic, so I'll go take care of that first."

"I'll be right behind you. I'm just going to clean up," Ash replied quickly.

"Perfect, see you in a few."

Shay drained her coffee and stood before hurrying out with a wave. Ash walked to the windows that looked out over the porch toward the path that led to the lodge. Beyond the lodge and over a small rise through the trees were the vet clinic, the rescue program, and the farmhouse where Ash grew up with Jackson.

Turning back, Ash walked to the table with her arms wrapped around her waist. "You can't stay for breakfast again," she whispered pointedly.

"No need to whisper, and why not? I don't think Shay suspected anything."

For some reason, I was feeling stubborn about Ash's insistence on secrecy. Maybe it was because I felt like it would infuriate Jackson less if I told him what was going on, rather than him finding out some other way. I hooked a finger in a belt loop and tugged her toward me. As soon as I got my other hand on her hip, I pulled her onto my lap.

"Don't worry about it," I murmured right before dropping kisses along her neck.

Ash's cheeks flushed when she bit her lip. "Mack," she whispered.

"What if I don't want us to be a secret anymore?" I asked before dipping my head and dusting kisses along her collarbone.

Ash went still in my lap. Lifting my head, I found her eyes wide with uncertainty flickering in their depths. I wanted to kick her ex-fiancé's ass. Ash didn't trust anyone, not even me. Maybe I wasn't worth it to her, but this thing with us was *good*. Really good.

"Mack, what do you want? I'm not all full of love and rainbows. It doesn't exactly go well for me. You're the guy who always plays it cool. I know we have hot sex, but if we tell all of our friends about that, well, it's really going to suck when it all blows up."

Her words hit me. Hard. Maybe I was falling for her, but that was a part of the problem. I didn't know how to do a relationship. When it came to those who mattered to me, the one and only time I'd let someone down had been an epic disaster.

I held her gaze quietly. "Okay. I won't push. If I come over tonight, you gonna let me in?"

Ash's soft sigh filtered through the cracks in my heart. Tucking her forehead into the center of my chest, she took several breaths. "I'm not particularly good at saying no to you. We have good orgasms," she teased.

"I deliver, sugar. I told you that," I managed to tease in return even though my heart was almost aching at the distance she was trying to create by teasing and keeping it light.

I left her behind to go to work, feeling unsettled inside.

Chapter Twenty-Two

ASH

Glancing behind me, I turned around just in time to find Squeaky nudging the back of my calf. A neighbor's little girl found the small pig on the side of the road only a few months before I'd left to travel. Leaning over, I fished a treat out of my pocket. "Here ya go, Squeaky," I said.

She gobbled it up, making a cute snuffling sound when she looked up at me afterward. "Everyone loves Gloria because she's a little more social than Squeaky, but I adore Squeaky," Shay said from across the aisle in the barn.

Straightening, I smiled. "I don't have a favorite, but Squeaky is precious. So you're training Mischief?" I asked.

Shay was leaning against a stall, her elbow resting on top of the half door as she stroked the pony's neck. Mischief had landed with our rescue program because we were one of the few that took in horses. He had almost died as a young colt. Known as a Banker pony, he'd been born as a wild pony on the Outer Banks. For the most part, the herds were left to their own, but occasionally, interventions occurred.

In Mischief's case, his mother was weak and ailing after giving birth. As a result, they were both near death. Because

Mischief was young, he was removed, and his mother went on to survive and thrive. He'd landed in our program, and Jackson decided to keep him. He lived up to his name and then some.

Shay smiled over at me. "Oh yeah, I love this little guy. He's fun."

"Have you tried riding him yet?"

"A few times. I'm taking it slow, and I'm so busy that slow is my only option," she said with a little laugh. "Shall we get started?"

At my nod, she gave Mischief a last stroke and pushed away from his stall to stride down the aisle between the barns. "Is this weird? I mean, this is your place too as much as it is Jackson's. Here I am now, showing you my system."

I rested a hand on my hip. "Shay, I've been gone for a year and a half. And honestly, organization has never been my strong suit. I love how you come up with a system for everything. Dani thinks you're a godsend. Between your help and Valentina managing all of our accounting, I feel like things are in much better shape than they ever were. Show me your system. Please. I'm great at following instructions."

Shay approached and threw her arms around me. She gave me a tight hug, and I returned it. She was my oldest friend, and we'd known each other for as long as I could remember.

Stepping back, I smiled. Shay knuckled a tear away from her eye. "Are you okay?" I asked, suddenly concerned.

Shay sniffled and smiled. "Yes. I just missed you. It's thanks to you that I'm even here, so it means a lot that you're finally back. I worried you might've thought I wasn't there enough for you for a while."

I knew she was referring to the situation with her abusive ex and how it'd driven a wedge between her and everyone. Lifting my hands, I squeezed her shoulders and looked straight into her eyes. "I was always there and just waiting for you. Don't ever think you were going to lose me as a friend."

Shay took a shaky breath and nodded. I gave her shoulders another squeeze and let my hands drop. "It's really good to be home."

Shay and I got the horses fed and settled for the evening before we crossed the pasture to the barn where all the other rescue animals stayed. The horse barn portion of the rescue was in the lower part of a barn built into a hillside. The upper floor was our vet clinic and had a parking lot entrance on the opposite side, giving us the ability to keep that traffic separate from the rescue and the lodge. The vet clinic and rescue program were located close to my family's old farmhouse while the lodge was over a small rise through the trees.

When we stepped into the rescue barn, Shay glanced over. "We got some puppies yesterday. Have you been out since then?"

"Oh, really?" I breathed. "I was tied up with appointments all afternoon and then helped Jackson with an emergency surgery."

Shay's face broke into a wide smile. "Come on, they're so freaking cute."

"How did we end up with puppies?" I mused as I followed her into the rescue barn.

Gloria was napping in her large stall with Squeaky. She lumbered to her feet and immediately walked out. Their stall was never left closed, so those two pretty much had the run of the farm and lodge.

I greeted her as I followed Shay to the room at the back of the barn. At the moment, we had Gloria and Squeaky who were permanent residents, along with our adopted opossum. We also had chickens outside, and a goat who'd been abandoned after destroying a room in a family's house.

Shay and I were quiet as we stepped through the door. This room was where we kept any injured rescues or in this case, a litter of adorable puppies. They were in a small pen, sleeping in a pile together.

I leaned over the railing and let out a sigh. "They are *so* cute." Reaching a hand out, I lightly stroked my fingers over one of the puppies. "How did we get them?"

"Apparently, somebody found them abandoned in a box in the restroom at the high school track. School's out for the summer, so it's just luck that somebody happened to stop and use that bathroom when they were there for a run."

"So sweet," she cooed as we both leaned over and shamelessly stared at them. One of the little puppies lifted its head and straightened on the pile of indistinguishable bundles of fur. The puppies were all brown. The puppy, a male, came toddling over on unsteady legs. His motion roused a few others, and Shay and I happily petted the cluster.

"So there're seven." Lifting one, I asked, "How old are you?"

"I brought Jackson out last night before we went to bed, and his guess is around seven weeks."

I inspected a few of them. "I'd say Jackson is about right. I hope whoever dumped them let them stay with mama until right before they did that. I'd prefer they weren't weaned until eight weeks, but they'll survive."

One of them was on the shy side and observed its littermates bumbling around while Shay and I laughed and petted them. I held a hand out toward the shy one in the corner. The puppy finally stood and approached my hand cautiously. "Oh, sweet pea." She followed my hand until I could scoop her up. The moment I held her close to my chest, she let out a soft little breath and nuzzled her head against my heart.

Shay glanced over. "I think you should keep her."

For a moment, I hesitated. Two years ago when I opened my phone and saw naked pictures of my ex with another woman, I'd just wanted to escape from the embarrassment of it all. I'd been living a temporary life in every way since then. Adopting a puppy was anything but temporary.

I couldn't really say why, but the idea of committing to something had anxiety spinning in my chest even though the temporary nature of my life had left me in a state of chronic anxiety and feeling unsettled. I *was* home, and I needed to find my way back to some sort of peace.

The sweet little puppy in my arms lifted her head and licked my chin, and my heart just turned into a blob of goo in my chest. "I'm keeping her."

Shay squealed. "Yay! One down, six to go."

"They're puppies. We're going to find homes for them fast." Looking down at the puppy, I asked, "What's your name?"

Her small tail thumped softly against my belly. "I'm going to have to think about it, and you're going to stay with your siblings for at least another week."

"That's what Jackson said."

"Yeah. With their mom would've been best, but this way, they've got that time of security with each other. I suppose we should feed everybody, huh?"

Shay nodded. "Let's start with them."

After we finished and were walking out of the barn with Gloria and Squeaky on our heels, I heard Mack's voice. My head whipped around so fast, it was embarrassing, and I hoped no one happened to be looking at me.

Mack and my brother were standing outside in the small paddock that led into the large pasture between the two barns. Fortunately, Jackson was looking at a notebook while Mack was pointing at something in it.

Shay, because she was ridiculously in love with my brother, wasn't paying the least bit of attention to me and was already trotting over to Jackson's side. I felt like an excited pony who wanted to gallop over to Mack.

Just as Jackson was sliding his arm around Shay's waist and leaning down to kiss her, Mack lifted his head. His eyes locked with mine across the distance separating us, and it felt like flames licked in the air between us.

Chapter Twenty-Three

MACK

Days, nights, and weeks kept passing. Every single one of those nights found me tangled up in bed with Ash. The pressure of keeping a secret I didn't want to keep was starting to feel heavy. Meanwhile, something else was happening.

All those years of finding it easy to keep things casual had me thinking I could manage this. If I was a master of anything, it was friends with benefits. It worked for me. *No complications, keep it casual, and don't worry about it.* I told myself that was how it should feel with Ash.

But it didn't. Not even a little. From the very first night I'd given in to the flames flickering between us, it was more. So much more.

I watched Ash play one night in Asheville. Most of our friends were there, and I'd had to batten down my reaction. Because watching her perform was seeing her without the walls she kept up. Every cell in my body felt electrified when her throaty voice rang out at the end of a song. And yet, I couldn't do anything about it then. I'd had to wait until she opened the door to her cabin hours later.

The thrum of my need for her began to take on more

intensity, more meaning, and more resulting confusion now that we were home. Home was filled with memories. Every time I turned around, memories slapped me right across the face.

When Evie looked over her shoulder, laughing at something I said one night in the staff kitchen at the lodge, her smile looked so much like Krista's that it felt like a jagged piece of metal driven into an old scar. There were so many landmarks I passed almost daily, each one of them holding a memory.

I had broken down the details of that day and that roughly ten-minute timeframe a thousand times in my mind. When you work as a first responder, you're constantly breaking down contingencies and making fast decisions. It was a habit for me. Every time I broke down the contingencies of that situation, there was no factor I could change that meant Krista lived in the overall equation. But the intellectual details were irrelevant in the emotional aftermath. My mind and my heart would never come to an agreement.

In my heart, I had failed. That was why I was terrified of falling for Ash or anyone for that matter. Yet I was oddly resigned because it was already happening. I'd stumbled and lost my balance completely. My fingers were slipping off the edge of control I was trying to cling to, yet it was far too late, and I was falling at a breathtaking speed for Ash.

While I was wrestling with my own ghosts, I was also frustrated with Ash and how hard she tried to pretend all we had was sex between us. When we were together at night, it was as if a cocoon sheltered us from the rest of the world and reality. The moment the sun broke through the darkness, she all but kicked me out and treated me the same way she treated everyone else.

About six weeks after we'd gotten back to Stolen Hearts Valley, I went with Jackson and a few of the other guys on the crew for a climbing workout. As bad luck would have it, Jackson came knocking on Ash's cabin door before I left.

Ash had given me her usual wide-eyed look whenever she worried anybody might notice anything. Masking my frustration, I shrugged. "Just having coffee, Ash. Not a crime."

When she opened the door, I called out, "Hey, man. Had to grab some coffee from Ash before I met you. My coffee's only adequate. Hers is incredible."

Jackson stood in the doorway in a pair of fitted climbing shorts and a T-shirt. He shrugged as he stepped through the door. "You aren't known for your kitchen skills," he offered with a hitch of his brows and a grin.

"Definitely not." I took a swallow of my coffee, my eyes tracking Ash as she nervously twisted a lock of hair around her finger.

"What's up?" she asked, her voice a little too forced and cheerful.

Jackson stopped at the edge of her kitchen counter and rested a hip against it. "Just stopped by to say hey. I was on my way to grab Mack, so it's handy he's here. I only have to knock on one door. We're headed up for a climb. Can you handle any emergencies at the clinic?" he asked, his eyes on Ash.

"Of course. You know I was doing vet work while I was traveling with the rodeo, right?"

"I know. Not doubting your skills, just making sure you're comfortable with it and feeling like you're back in the swing of things," he replied.

Ash lifted her coffee cup off the counter. "I know, I know. Didn't mean to get defensive."

"Good, because there's no need for that. I'm so damn happy you're back. You have no idea. And it's not just because of the vet clinic."

Ash smiled, leaning over to bump him lightly on the shoulder with her fist. "I know. I'm glad to be here. Go have fun with your climbing and don't you even worry about the clinic. I have it totally covered."

"Awesome." Jackson's gaze shifted to me. "You ready to roll?"

I stood from the table, draining the last of my coffee. "Absolutely."

Just as I was trying to decide if I should put the cup in the sink, Ash pushed away from the counter and reached for it. "I'll take that."

"Thanks for the coffee." I wished I could kiss her goodbye for the day, but that was not an option. Most definitely not in front of Jackson.

————

An hour or so later, I paused along the trail and glanced at Wade who was right behind me. "This way, right?"

Wade looked in the direction I was pointing, which was a narrow, not very well-traveled trail, an offshoot from the main trail we were following into the mountains.

"Think so," Wade said with a quick chuckle. "Your memory's better than mine."

Jackson caught up with us. "Mack was always the smart one in school. His memory is like a fucking steel trap."

"It's not that good. Things just stick in my brain."

Lucas, who was bringing up the rear, stopped beside us where we were clustered on the trail. "Yeah, this is the one. It leads to a great climbing face. Not too busy either."

"Alright, lead the way," Jackson said with a nod in my direction.

The narrow trail eventually widened and offered a vista out over Stolen Hearts Valley. I paused and just absorbed the view. The Blue Ridge Mountains were home for me. Despite the ghosts of one memory crowding my thoughts, it was good to be here. My soul felt settled here in a way I didn't feel no matter where else I was.

The rising sun illuminated the bright, clear sky over the mountains. Turning around, I saw Lucas and Jackson already tugging climbing gear out of their backpacks. Wade was busy chowing down on a breakfast bar.

"Give me some of that," I said as I strode to stand beside him.

He promptly broke it in half and handed me half. "Ash didn't feed you breakfast?" he teased.

Aw, fuck. I knew by the look in Wade's eyes that he knew something was up with Ash and me.

He winked. "Don't worry, I won't say anything. Dani's the one who noticed. You know she gets to the restaurant every day before five."

I stuffed a giant bite of the breakfast bar in my mouth and nodded. After swallowing, I replied, "Thanks for keeping it quiet."

The four of us settled into an easy rhythm of climbing. This particular cliff face was high enough and wide enough for several routes for climbing. Wade and I paired up for the first hour or so, and then we switched out, and I paired with Jackson.

I didn't sense any shift in his attitude toward me, which was why my jaw nearly came unhinged as he was helping me organize the ropes after our last climb. Lucas was busy belaying while Wade rappelled down.

"So what's up with you and Ash?"

Jackson wasn't even looking in my direction when my head whipped around to look toward him. He lifted his eyes just in time to see me with my mouth wide open.

"Oh, fuck," he muttered.

"What do you mean?" I finally asked in return.

Jackson straightened with a length of climbing rope in his palm as he began to wind the line into a tidy figure eight. "I'm not stupid, Mack. I know you've been staying at her cabin. That's not counting me running into you there this morning."

I took a breath, my cheeks puffing out before I let it go. Leaning my head back, I stared pointlessly at the sky, idly noticing clouds gathering. Any minute now, the sun would be blotted out. It looked like a thunderstorm was on the way sometime this afternoon.

Leveling my eyes with Jackson's again, I said, "Ash doesn't want me to say anything. That wasn't my preference."

A muscle clenched in Jackson's jaw. Although I'd known the guy forever, he had a damn good poker face. I wasn't even sure if he was angry. Not at first.

"I know Ash would kick my ass if she heard I had an opinion about this, but what the fuck?" He finished winding the climbing rope, and his fist curled around it tightly as he stepped closer. "She's been through enough, Mack."

Okay, so he was angry. I could deal with that. Nodding, I straightened my shoulders. "I know. It's not what you think. If you need to hit me, go ahead."

Jackson rolled his eyes. "I'm only going to hit you if you hurt Ash. I'm not an idiot, but I *am* fucking pissed. And what the hell do you mean it's not what I think?"

Just then, Lucas's voice came from behind us. "What's up, guys?"

"Mack's got a thing going with Ash, and he couldn't be bothered to tell me about it," Jackson said, his voice low and controlled.

I felt Lucas stop beside me and slid my eyes sideways. His alert gaze bounced from me to Jackson and back again. "I don't have an opinion on this, but if y'all are going to fight, maybe we should do it where one of you can't fall off a cliff," he said, his tone dry.

Wade approached, draining a water bottle before looking amongst us. He met my eyes, a knowing look in his. He blessedly remained silent.

"We're not gonna fight, but Mack better tell me what he means," Jackson said flatly, his gaze trained on mine.

Fuck me. Ash was going to kill me. But I wasn't going to lie to her older brother who also happened to be one of my best friends.

I took a breath before replying, "I like Ash. She means something to me."

"What the fuck does that mean?" Jackson countered. "Do you want to be serious with her? Did you even think about the fact that she just got out of a relationship?"

Anxiety churned in my gut. I knew Jackson's questions were, well, logical. The problem was I didn't have all the answers.

I stared back at Jackson for a beat and then simply told the truth. "Look, I didn't plan this. All I know is she means a lot to me. I would've told you sooner, but she got pissed off when I suggested it."

Jackson let out a muttered curse. "You'd better not fucking hurt her." He turned and started stuffing the climbing gear in a backpack.

Chapter Twenty-Four

ASH

Resting my hips against a stool, I watched as Dani rolled a ball of dough into a thin sheet and began cutting it into triangles. She spooned filling into them before twisting them closed.

"Want some help?" I asked.

Dani glanced up, dragging her wrist across her forehead to get an errant curl out of her eyes. "Nope. I got it. I'll be done in just a minute. Just making enough for us back here. You can get me a glass of wine," she added with a quick grin.

"Coming right up." I stood and strode over to the counter running along the wall where there was a wine rack underneath. "White or red?" I called over my shoulder.

"I'll take white. It's been so hot today."

I snagged a glass and a bottle of white wine before returning to the table. "Know who else will be joining us tonight?" I asked as I filled her glass and returned the cork to the bottle.

"It's always mix or match. I figure the guys will be here. Wade texted me that they're on their way back from the climb. No wine for you?" she asked when I sipped the glass of water I'd gotten earlier.

I shrugged. "Nah. My stomach's been a little weird the past few days. I know it's old news around here, but you and Wade, huh?"

Dani put the last pastry on a baking tray and looked over at me. Her cheeks pinkened slightly with her smile. "Yeah, me and Wade."

"That was a long time coming."

Walking across the kitchen, Dani slid the tray of pastries in the oven. She pulled out another tray and returned to the large stainless-steel table where she was working. Setting it down, she replied, "It was, but we had to get there the way we did."

"I'm happy for y'all. Really. How are things?"

"With me and Wade?"

"Yes. I want to hear all the good stuff."

Dani flushed a deeper shade of pink and laughed softly. "Things are actually really great. We're looking to find a house and move away from the lodge, hopefully soon."

"You're still going to run the kitchen, right?" I teased.

Dani laughed again. "Of course. You and Jackson are stuck with me forever. We just need more space."

"Works for me. What are those?" I asked, pointing a finger toward the tray of pastries cooling on the table between us.

"Ham pinwheels. Help yourself." She reached for a napkin from the center of the table and put one on it before handing it over. "Careful, it's hot." I set it on the table to give it a minute. "Now, how are you and Mack?" she asked, taking me entirely off guard.

I hoped like hell I didn't blush too hard. I took another swallow of water to buy myself a little time. Shrugging, I replied, "I'm fine. Mack is fine. We had a good trip."

Dani drummed her fingertips on the table. "Your arm

looks good." Her eyes flicked down to my forearm where I'd been burned.

Glancing down, I trailed a fingertip over the pink and freshly healed skin. "Yep, it's all healed."

Dani stared at me for a moment, her perceptive gaze making me want to squirm. Even though I didn't want to say it out loud, I *knew* that *she* knew something was up with Mack and me. I traced my fingertip around the rim of my glass, prepared to wait her out. I didn't have to wait too long.

"All right, I'll just say it. I know Mack's been staying at your place. I've seen him leaving several times in the morning."

"Oh hell," I muttered. "You're not gonna buy that he was just there for coffee?" Oh, how I wished she would, but Dani was no fool.

Dani rolled her eyes. "Uh, no. Plus, there's a vibe."

Leaning my head back, I stared at the ceiling for a moment before bringing my eyes back to hers. "Does Jackson know? Have you said anything to anyone?"

"Of course not. Well, I did mention it to Wade, but he won't say anything. He might give Mack some hell about it, but that's it. I swore him to secrecy. Him getting laid as much as he wants relies on him honoring my wishes," she offered with a sly smile.

I burst out laughing at that. "Of course it does." I sighed. "Why can't anything stay private around here?"

Dani shrugged. "I get it. Even though I'm the one calling you out on Mack, I'm trying to do you a favor before rumors get out. I tried to keep things quiet with Wade, and it wasn't very successful. But seriously, what's the deal with you and Mack?"

In a way, I was relieved Dani knew because I needed someone to talk to. Dani was a good friend and as solid as they came. "When we saw each other again, there was some serious chemistry. I'll be the first to tell you it surprised the hell out of me. As long as I've known Mack, there was never a spark. We weren't like you and Wade where we had a thing in high school. I tried not to do anything about it, but that was a total fail. I think we both thought it would burn out."

"Let me guess. It hasn't," Dani said with a wide grin.

"Oh, no. He's, um, pretty great in bed."

Dani threw her head back with a laugh. "I bet he is."

I started twirling a lock of hair nervously around my finger before dropping it quickly. "I'm being stupid. I always fall for the wrong guys, and Mack is not long-term material."

Dani shrugged. "He's a great guy. Maybe it'll work out with you two. Is that what you want?" she asked, going dead serious so fast it put me on notice just how unsettled I was inside.

"I don't know what I want. I don't want to be stupid, and I'm tired of making bad decisions. Everything blew up with Brian, and then I got involved with Kyle. He was cute, but let's just say his talents in bed didn't live up to the zing. I got tired of being a side piece, for lack of a better way to put it. I was an idiot. I don't know why I thought I could do the stupid friends-with-benefits thing. There's nothing wrong with it, but it doesn't suit my personality."

"Kyle was an asshole," Dani said flatly.

I sighed. "I know you mean well, but that just kind of makes me feel like shit," I said softly, fighting the wave of shame that rolled through me.

Dani practically ran around the table between us and pulled me into a tight and fierce hug. "Oh, honey," she said as she stepped back. "I didn't mean it like that. I get it. I'm protective of you, and I didn't like the way he treated you, even if he didn't want to be serious. I want someone to love you exactly how you should be loved because you're my friend and you deserve to be treated better. That's all."

"It's good to be home," I commented.

"Of course it is. We all missed you."

The door from the hallway in the back opened, and Shay came walking in. "Hey y'all," she called.

"Hey," Dani and I returned in unison.

"Do you happen to know what time the guys are getting here?" Dani asked as she turned away to check on the oven.

"Jackson just called. Probably a half hour. I guess they have a meeting at the station. They're reviewing the on-call schedule."

Shay slipped onto a stool across the table from me. "Is there more wine?"

Dani called over her shoulder," Of course! You know where the glasses are."

Shay hopped up again and strolled over to the counter along the wall, fetching another glass. Once she was seated again and filling her wine glass, she looked over at me. "So, when were you planning to tell us?"

"Tell you what?"

Dani returned to the table with a basket of bread and a bowl of artichoke dip. She glanced back and forth between us, and added, "You can't keep secrets very long around here, but you already know that."

I closed my eyes and let out a groan. Opening them, I met Shay's gaze, feeling my cheeks flame. "Oh God, if you know, does that mean Jackson knows?"

"He just called me," she said, casting me a glare. "If you'd given me a heads-up, I could've managed the situation."

"How the hell does he know?"

"Look, he already suspected something was up. He confronted Mack about it, and Mack fessed up. He assures me he didn't hit Mack."

"Oh God," I repeated before taking a gulp of water. "Look, it's no big deal."

Shay held my eyes for a moment, understanding softening her gaze. "You know none of us would judge you, right?"

"I know, it's just—" I snatched a piece of bread from the basket and scooped some dip onto it.

Shay did the same, giving me the moment to collect

myself. Dani, always on the move, was over checking on something.

"I didn't plan on it," I said after I finished chewing. "And I'm not really sure what I would call what we're doing."

"Jackson thinks Mack really likes you."

Dani returned with a tray of pizza and slid it between Shay and me on the table. "That's what I thought," she chimed in.

"We're friends. Of course he likes me." I stuffed another piece of bread with artichoke dip in my mouth. "This is ah-maz-ing," I said with my mouth full.

"Everything Dani makes is amazing," Shay added. "That's not what Jackson meant when he said he thinks Mack really likes you. He thinks he *likes* you, likes you."

"I have the worst luck with men."

Shay shrugged, waving a hand dismissively. "So what? I could say the same until Jackson."

"I know," I said, instantly feeling like I was exaggerating my own situation." I didn't mean—"

She shook her head quickly. "Oh God, don't apologize about thinking you had worse luck than me. Just because your fiancé wasn't abusive doesn't mean he wasn't an asshole. Brian was cheating on you, and you got naked pictures of it. And Kyle was just a player. I sure hope he was incredible in bed."

I rolled my eyes. "His skills were not worth all the trouble."

"How about Mack's skills?" Shay teased.

My cheeks instantly got hot, and my friends burst out laughing.

Chapter Twenty-Five

MACK

Leaning toward the center of the table, I picked up the platter of seasoned potatoes. After I served myself, I felt Ash's eyes on me. When I lifted my head, my gaze collided with hers. I wasn't totally sure how to read it, but I was confident she was pissed with me. Considering we were surrounded by friends, I couldn't do a damn thing about it now.

"Hey, can you pass that my way?" Dawson asked, elbowing me in the side

I lifted the platter again and handed it over, replying, "Words work, you know."

"Dude, you were zoned out staring at Ash. I think my elbow was necessary," Dawson quipped.

I didn't dare look in Ash's direction now. Instead, I rolled my eyes. "Whatever," I muttered before stuffing a bite of garlic bread in my mouth. Fortunately, anything Dani made was thoroughly distracting. I focused on my food rather than Ash's mood. I finished chewing and let out a satisfied sigh before glancing at Dani. "That is some fine garlic bread."

"Seriously," Wade affirmed. He leaned over and dusted a kiss on her cheek. "But everything you make is good."

Dawson snorted beside me. "Ever since those two kissed and made up, we are treated daily to Wade being a total sap."

Grace, who didn't happen to be waitressing in the restaurant tonight, cast a grin at Dawson. "You're a sap about Evie."

Boone chuckled. Ash stabbed her fork into her salad, her gaze arcing around the table. "Seems like it's a table full of saps these days. I go away for a year and a half, and everybody falls in love."

Jackson's eyes lingered on me for a beat, but he stayed quiet. I silently let my breath go. Ash was going to find out Jackson knew about us one way or another, so I knew I'd have to face the music. I just preferred not to do so in a group setting, especially not *this* group setting. Too many people here were too comfortable sharing their opinion about their friends' private lives.

I was happy to be home because it was good to be back around friends I'd known for years. But the downside was they all had opinions.

For example, Dawson. "Well, I'd say it's your turn then," he offered. He popped a bite of bread in his mouth as he glanced from Ash to me. "Geez, y'all are the only two single people at the table."

Dani choked on a bite, and Wade whacked her helpfully between the shoulder blades. When she kept coughing, he handed over a glass of water.

I was relieved for the noisy interruption because it took the attention away from Ash and me. When I looked over at her again, she was studiously focused on eating. I didn't like the tension emanating from her and was restless for this dinner to end so I could try to talk to her.

It didn't take long for the group to start drifting apart. Grace took off to cover the last half of the dinner shift in the restaurant, and Dani hurried back into the restaurant kitchen. Eventually, the only people left were Jackson, Shay, Dawson, Wade, Ash, and me. Wade was talking with Dawson about something over by the door that led into the back offices. I was carrying plates to the dishwasher when I felt a hand on my shoulder.

Glancing back, I found Jackson. "What's up?" I asked before I resumed walking as he fell into stride beside me.

"Are you gonna let Ash know I know?" he asked.

Talk about fucking awkward. I seriously did *not* want to chat with Jackson about my intimate relationship with his sister. I was relieved to have my hands full. I reached the industrial dishwasher and began putting the plates in the large rack. "Of course," I finally said.

Jackson must have sensed my irritation. "You know, I could be a hell of a lot more pissed off about this."

Setting the last plate in the rack, I lifted the stainless-steel coil sprayer and rinsed my hands under the scalding hot water. I snagged a clean towel from a stack on the shelf directly above the dishwasher to dry my hands, then turned and looked at Jackson. "I know. I just would've preferred to do this at my own pace."

Jackson's eyes held mine before he gave a sharp nod. "I get it. I'm just concerned. Hell, you know Remy is one of my best friends too, and he wasn't thrilled when Shay and I got together," he began, referring to Shay's older brother who we'd all grown up with. Remy had moved away to Alaska a few years ago. "I get it, so I'm not trying to be a total asshole. Ash didn't handle it well when things blew up right before her wedding, and I don't think this year and a half away with Kyle has helped matters. Fucking idiot," he muttered under his breath.

Because Jackson was my friend, and I respected him, I took a breath and answered him honestly. "I'm not exactly a poster boy for commitment. I don't know what Ash wants, but I don't intend to hurt her." I opened my mouth to say more but caught myself.

Because I couldn't fucking believe what I almost said. I almost told him I loved her. I supposed I did.

Jackson's eyes penetrated mine, and a sense of unease prickled through me. He knew me as well as anyone did, so at that moment, I sensed he knew the truth of my feelings for Ash, though he was kind enough not to put me on the spot and force me to admit them.

After a moment, he gave the slightest incline of his head. "Okay. I trust you. Don't ask me to sit on this forever. Wade knows, Dani figured it out, and Shay already suspected it."

"I know. I'm planning to talk to Ash later tonight."

My plan to talk to Ash went from later to much later when our team got an emergency call just as I was about to leave the lodge.

———

"A group of teens partying in a boat. That's a recipe for disaster," Jackson said right after he dropped his cell phone on the seat. "Obviously, an accident happened. Apparently, the 911 call came in about ten minutes ago. It took them a few minutes to ping a location because the cell reception is shitty there."

He was driving, deftly maneuvering his truck along the narrow mountain road. He'd slapped the emergency light on the roof when we took off from the lodge. By my count, four emergency vehicles were converging at the base of a trail that led to a popular area for canoeing. The sky was inky black.

Bitter tension coated the insides of my stomach, and my chest felt cold. I'd cut my teeth as a first responder in training out West responding to fires. They're the hotshots who went in and beat back the flames. The first responders came in the next wave to deal with anybody injured. I'd done some river rescues along the roaring and famed Colorado River.

Yet a ghost, just one, was coming back to haunt me tonight. Krista died along a different stretch of the very river where we were headed tonight. She, too, had been fooling around on a boat, just as so many kids did back when we were growing up. A fall overboard when they went over a rough patch of water in the river had slammed her head into the side of the boat, and she died almost instantly. Or so they said. My mind—the irrational, wishful, grieving part of my brain—still clung to the idea that maybe if I'd been right there, I could've gotten her out of the water and done CPR fast enough that she would've lived.

To this day, the voice of one of the EMTs echoed through my thoughts. *"She didn't feel anything. It was that fast. And just remember, you can't change what happened."*

The fucking past. There were so many things I could change. Apparently, the past wasn't on that list, and I doubted whether I'd ever truly get past this lingering guilt.

"Mack," Jackson said, his voice just loud enough to knock me off the rails of that train of thought.

"Yeah?" I slid my gaze sideways. His eyes were trained on the road, which was a good thing because we were hauling ass on a side dirt road now.

"That was only the third time I said your name. You okay?"

Jackson didn't need to say out loud what I knew he meant. We'd both been there that day, but Krista wasn't his little sister. My guilt was compounded. All my life growing up, it was my younger twin sisters—Evie and Krista—and me. Not only had I failed to keep Krista safe, but Evie had lost her twin. I knew how tight they'd been. It was an almost spiritual bond. Evie lost more than I did, and I felt guilty for that too.

With my gut twisting sickly, I looked ahead at the road in front of us illuminated by Jackson's headlights. "Yeah, I'm okay. I've done a few river rescues."

"Because you could say you weren't if you really weren't," Jackson added.

"I'm really fine," I insisted, lying through my teeth. I was hoping my instincts and training would just kick in once we got there.

In short order, we were there, standing on a rocky ledge overlooking the dark river. At the base of this ledge was a curved section along the river with a grassy stretch that led to a popular camping area. There were only two ways to get there—rappelling down this ledge or by boat.

We didn't have time to go by water, which might be the only thing that kept me sane. Our crew was quickly assembling with Jackson taking the lead on climbing along with Walker. Dawson and I would rappel down after them, and the others would set up a medical station up here once we figured out what we needed.

When my feet landed lightly on the rocky ledge below, and I could feel the rush of cooler air from the cold mountain river running by, memories came at me hard and fast. I ignored them all and turned. I needed to move because that was the only thing that was going to get me through this.

Chapter Twenty-Six

ASH

"It's a river rescue?" Evie asked.

Shay looked over at her and nodded. Evie's brow knitted with worry, and she leaned over to pick up a puppy from the pile gamboling around on the floor.

After the emergency call came in, Shay had asked if I wanted to go check on the puppies with her. Of course I did. Anything for a distraction. Over an hour had passed since then with no updates. We were in the reception area at the vet clinic with a blanket spread in the middle of the floor for the puppies. Evie had joined us after the restaurant closed.

Shay caught my eyes, concern held in hers. I was probably as worried about Mack as Evie was. Evie had lost her twin sister in the very same accident that haunted Mack. He never spoke of it, but Evie seemed more at peace about it.

"Are you okay?" I finally asked as I reached for the puppy I planned to take home sometime in the next few days. I'd named her Betty.

Evie looked over and lifted a puppy onto her lap. "I'm just worried about Mack. I know he's done a few river rescues out West, but y'all know what happened. He's never admitted it, but I always thought he stayed away from Stolen Hearts because of what happened. It really messed with him, and now he's dealing with a rescue in the same river where Krista died."

Anxiety spun madly in my chest, making it hard to get a breath. I looked at the little puppy in my lap. Her eyes were liquid brown. "He's going to be okay, right?" I mused to Betty.

"Mack *is* going to be okay," Shay said firmly as she looked from Evie to me. "I'm sure this is stressful, but it's good he came home. Running never solves anything."

When Shay looked toward me again, I knew she was thinking about what was going on with Mack and me. From my conversation earlier with Dani, I knew they'd discussed it.

Here I sat with Evie, Mack's sister, and I felt like I was keeping secrets from her, along with Jackson. Even though I now knew Jackson knew, we hadn't discussed it. Cuddling Betty in my lap, I looked over at Evie. "I should let you know something."

Evie brushed her dark hair off her shoulders as her blue eyes lifted to mine. Her eyes were so similar to Mack's—that bottomless ocean blue. I had no idea how she was going to feel about this. In spite of my nervousness, I knew this likely wouldn't be as loaded of a topic for her as it was for Jackson.

"Mack and I kind of have a thing."

Evie burst out laughing. "I suspected as much." Her gaze sobered almost instantly. "You're probably as worried about him as I am, huh?"

I shrugged. "Maybe, maybe not. Things like that are relative. Obviously, I'm worried for him, but he doesn't really discuss what happened with Krista. At all."

Evie looked down at another puppy who waddled over and bumped into her knee. She pulled it onto her lap with the other one. "Is it serious with you two? Mack hasn't said a word to me about it."

I heard Shay's huff of a laugh and looked over to see her rolling her eyes.

"What's that for?" I asked, feeling uncomfortable.

"I don't think Mack talked to anybody about it until Jackson confronted him today," she returned.

"What?" I asked.

Evie bit her lip and shook her head. "And you were worried about keeping it from me. I'm Mack's little sister, and I'm not likely to get all tied up over who he's getting naked with. Your brother probably has a different opinion."

"Ugh," I groaned.

Shay held my eyes and sighed. "You seriously thought people didn't notice? Jackson asked me about it before. Then he stopped by your place when he was going to pick up Mack this morning, and apparently, Mack was there. The first time Jackson asked me, it was because he caught Mack staring at you. He's no idiot, none of us are. When you're not looking, Mack pretty much always has his eyes on you. I don't know how you feel, but Mack's totally got a thing for you."

I looked down at Betty. The sweet puppy didn't care how confused I was about Mack. "I guess I am an idiot." Bringing my eyes up to my friends, I shrugged. "I don't know. I never had a thing for Mack before, never. Then, well, there was a spark when we saw each other." I let out a breath, my cheeks puffing with air before I released it. "I wasn't looking for anything serious, and I don't think Mack was. Now, apparently everyone knows."

"What do you want?" Shay asked softly.

My throat felt tight, and it wasn't just about Mack. I was just really good at being epically stupid when it came to men. Swallowing through the emotion knotting in my throat, I shrugged again. "Honestly, I don't know. I'm afraid I might be hoping for something more, and I don't think that's smart."

"Mack is the best kind of guy," Evie said, and I heard the protectiveness in her tone.

"I know he is. That's not what I mean. It's just that I don't have the best track record. Mack didn't make me any promises, so I don't have any expectations. But I know he usually keeps things very casual. I know he's a great guy, Evie. I'm worried I'm in over my head. It's like my baggage collides with his."

Evie was quiet, understanding dawning in her eyes. "I get it. It was kind of like that for me with Dawson at first until we figured it out. Obviously, Mack hasn't talked to me about you, but for what it's worth, I don't believe you're just a fling to him. I think you mean something."

"How would you know that?" I didn't even try to keep the skepticism out of my voice, although my heart was spinning in circles and hope was trying to scream out to be heard over the doubts crowding my mind.

"Because of the way he looks at you," Shay and Evie replied almost instantaneously.

Shay's cell phone vibrated. She lifted it from the floor where it rested by her hip. "Oh, it's Jackson. Maybe we have an update."

———

Walking through the trees in the darkness, I tried to calm myself. Jackson had called to say everyone was safe, but it would be a while before they got back. I thought about my conversation with Shay and Evie. I was falling for Mack, and I was panicking. I didn't want him to think I had expectations. I didn't want to make the same mistake I made before. Although it was the naked texts that I never wanted to see that blew my wedding up, one detail was burned in my brain. It played on a loop in my thoughts in the aftermath of calling off my wedding.

Brian told me he wasn't ready, and he'd only asked me to

marry him because he felt pressured. By *me*. When I protested and told him I never said I wanted him to ask me to marry him, he reminded me that I gushed about other weddings and about what I wanted for our wedding. I *had* done that and had wanted us to get married. I'd been impatient and didn't really know why in hindsight.

Like so many girls in high school, my self-esteem slipped and stumbled. It fell even further in college. It didn't really matter why. I'd craved feeling wanted enough. After everything fell apart so spectacularly with Brian and swearing I didn't want to get serious, I just had to go and get a little crush on Kyle, player and friends-with-benefits extraordinaire. I thought I could be cool and deal with it.

In all honesty, I'd never even come close to falling for Kyle. He was too immature and impressed with himself for that. I had, however, learned the casual scene wasn't a good fit for me. My pride alone had kept me from coming home.

It hadn't helped matters at all that my fiancé ended up marrying the very woman who'd sent me the naked texts. Thank God she hadn't been a friend. Pressure or not, he just hadn't wanted me that way.

I didn't want to blow this any more spectacularly than I already had. I never meant to fall for Mack, but now I felt like I was in a free fall.

He brought all of this into sharp focus. I hated what he might be feeling trying to handle a rescue on the river where his little sister died.

I was going to be an adult about this, though, and stop running. I wasn't sure where this was going, but I never wanted him to feel pressured. I would face whatever happened. Returning to my quiet cabin, I wondered when Mack would be home.

Chapter Twenty-Seven

MACK

My worst fears proved to be unfounded. Although Krista was never far from my thoughts that night during those long hours, my instincts from training kicked in. No one died. There were several injuries to deal with and a complicated rescue that involved ferrying people up the cliff face in supported stretchers. At one point, we contemplated whether a transport by boat would be quicker but ruled it out due to time and darkness. This river wasn't an easy river to traverse in the daylight, so trying to do it in the dark would only make it more treacherous.

As predicted, it had been a boat full of high school boys, and every last one of them was drunk. One of them sustained a head injury when the boat crashed into the rocks, and another had broken his shoulder when he tumbled forward from the impact and jammed it against the steering wheel. Another had a nasty gash on his arm, but nobody seemed to know where he got it. They were all too drunk to be much use in questioning.

On the ride back, Jackson commented, "You said you were fine, and you were."

We didn't talk further. I was fucking tired, and I knew he was too. Those of us handling the climbing duties must've gone up and down that cliff ten times. Not to mention the strength it took to lift a stretcher on ropes. Anchors and pulleys helped, but all of it was hard work.

We were also wet, all of us soaked to the skin. Although it was a summer night, the mountain river was still icy cold. I figured a hot shower was the only thing that would thaw me out. Although I was relieved I'd kept my shit together tonight, somehow this rescue had tripped a switch in my brain. I'd been stumbling into this thing with Ash. I knew, I fucking *knew* I was falling in love with her. Hell, I was far past falling. My heart had crash-landed.

Yet I couldn't trick myself into thinking I could be the man she needed. Ever since Krista died, this belief that I just couldn't quite be enough had always clung to me.

Intellectually, I knew the bullshit my parents said in the aftermath hadn't helped and wasn't right. But your heart didn't always listen to your head.

Whenever I thought of my family, it was my younger twin sisters and me. We were the unit that stuck together. My parents had not been so great and were barely there emotionally. More than once, most vividly the night that Krista died, my mother had said, "You were supposed to be watching her."

I was supposed to be watching her. I *was* watching her, but just like that, it didn't matter. She was gone. Forever.

So how could I believe I could be the man Ash needed? She'd already been let down. Now, I also had to worry about letting Jackson down after promising him I wouldn't hurt her.

Tangled up in all of this was Ash, the only person I wanted to see tonight. I wanted to take a hot shower and lose myself in the fire that never failed to make me forget everything else.

A while later, I waved good night to Jackson at the farmhouse and walked through the trees along the lighted path. My feet kept on walking past my place because Ash was home. I could see the lights flickering through the trees.

Just one more night.

I knocked lightly on her door, hooking my hand over the doorframe above. I shouldn't be this nervous to see her, but my heart was pounding as hard as it had the first night when I finally gave in to my need for her.

The door swung open. For a second, I thought my heart was actually going to leap out of my chest. She stood there with her rich brown hair in a messy bun. Her eyes were bright under the light on her porch. She wore a tank top and a pair of sweatpants that hung low on her hips.

Everything I did was instinct when it came to her. Dropping my hand from above, I trailed my knuckles lightly along the sliver of exposed skin below her shirt. I needed to touch her that badly.

"Hey," she said, her eyes coasting over my face. "You're all wet."

My heart squeezed tight like a fist clenching. She tugged me inside, her hands quick as she began pulling at my wet clothes.

"Jackson just called to say y'all were back. Were you in the river all this time?"

I didn't really answer other than a murmured assent. In a minute, we were standing in the bathroom, and all I had left on were my boxers. Ash turned the shower on, and steam began to fill the room.

"You're cold. Come on, get in," she ordered.

"You too," I said.

Her brow furrowed with her puzzled look, but she didn't hesitate. After a second, she shimmied out of her sweatpants and dropped her tank top on the floor. Next thing I knew, she was shoving my boxers down and gave a little surprised squeak when my cock sprang free, thick with arousal.

I was driven solely by the need to lose myself in her.

Cupping her jaw, I stepped close and fit my mouth over hers, claiming her with a deep kiss.

Ash murmured something when I lifted my head for air. "You're cold," she repeated before pushing me into the shower under the hot water raining down.

She was right. I was clammy cold. The steaming water heated me quickly. When I saw the soap bubbles rolling over her skin, I lifted her against me, pressing her back against the tiled shower wall.

In one surge, I was buried inside her. I could finally forget all the punishing, painful memories I'd been holding at bay for too long.

———

The following morning, I belatedly remembered I'd been planning to tell Ash about my conversation with Jackson. We were having coffee at the kitchen table, a mundane morning activity that had become a habit. I loved it. The moment I thought about Jackson, I recalled just how close I'd been to telling Jackson I was in love with Ash.

Ash stood to refill her cup of coffee and glanced over her shoulder. "Do you need some?"

Sunlight cast through the window, glinting on her hair, and I wanted to drag her back to bed for a replay of last night. Instead, I said, "Always."

She laughed softly and crossed the room to snag my coffee cup off the table. A moment later, she set my cup in front of me and sat down with hers. When I met her eyes, I saw uncertainty flickering there. I waited because I sensed she had something to say.

After a sip of coffee, she bit her lip and then spoke. "So, uh, I found out Jackson knows about us."

I didn't know whether to be relieved or concerned that she beat me to the punch. When she stayed quiet for a moment, I offered, "He confronted me about it yesterday. I meant to tell you last night, but that was before the whole rescue happened. It wasn't really on my mind when I came home last night."

Her eyes searched my face before she nodded. "Are you okay? You don't talk about it, but I know it was probably hard to do a river rescue on that river."

For a split second, my lungs seized, but my heart kept on beating. I'd done the hard thing last night, so I could certainly handle this. "I'm fine. Really."

Ash took a swallow of her coffee. When she set her mug down, she began tracing the inside loop of the handle with her fingertip. Her eyes fell away before lifting again. "Mack, I know we don't talk much about whatever it is that we're doing, but I just want you to know I don't have any expectations."

My confusion must have been evident on my face. "About us," she added. "I just thought you should know that."

I genuinely wasn't sure how to respond, so all I said was, "Okay."

We finished our coffee. Jackson texted me to tell me the contractor who was pouring the concrete for the foundation for the new barn was early and asked if I could meet him over at the site.

I left feeling unsettled. As I walked through the trees, the only conclusion I could form regarding Ash's comment about no expectations was that she didn't think she could expect much from me.

Chapter Twenty-Eight

ASH

"Come here," I said as I leaned down and held my palm flat with a small treat on it.

Betty looked up from the squeaky toy she had been gifted by Shay and trotted across the kitchen floor to me. After she gobbled up the treat, I sat cross-legged on the floor and pulled her onto my lap.

The day after I told Mack I didn't have any expectations, I brought Betty home. Although I didn't know it at the time, that choice turned out to be prescient. I needed the company because Mack had gone from stopping over almost every night to only coming by twice, in an entire week.

Of course, the two times he'd been here had ended with us twined together skin to skin. Yet somehow, it felt as if an invisible barrier had fallen between us.

Having an adorable, snuggly, and demanding puppy kept me occupied. Betty started gnawing on one of my fingers, her sharp little teeth stinging. Leaning over, I reached for her squeaky toy, which she promptly began chewing.

"Are you ready to go to work?" I asked as I stood with her in my arms.

She replied by giving her toy a little shake. Setting her back down on the floor, I went to the bathroom and pulled on a pair of jeans and a T-shirt to wear to the clinic. I had two surgeries today. Fortunately, I would drop Betty off with the remaining two puppies still waiting for a home. The group would hang out in the reception area in the little playpen we'd set up.

As I walked past Mack's cabin, my stomach felt hollow. For weeks, I'd been worried about anyone noticing he was spending his nights with me. Now, I wondered what it was about me telling him I had no expectations that drove a wedge between us.

I heard his door opening after I walked beyond his cabin. I had to willfully keep from looking over my shoulder.

"Ash!" he called as I heard his footsteps moving at a slow jog behind me.

Stopping in the path, I waited. "Hey," I said, hoping my tone came out as casually as I intended. I wasn't bothered, not at all, that he hadn't been with me every night. I knew three of those nights the crew had been called out on rescues, so I was sure that was why. That had to be it.

Riiiight.

It's more likely you gave him the permission he was waiting for.

Mack's eyes met mine, his smile uncertain. My heart squeezed as I looked up. I missed being held by his strong arms every night.

"How's she doing?" he asked as he reached over to rub his fingers over her back and then let her chew on his thumb.

"Pretty good. I have enough things for her to chew so she hasn't destroyed anything she isn't supposed to yet. We're working on the potty training."

His smile reached his eyes this time. "Good to hear." We walked in silence for a few moments, and Mack stuffed his hands in his pockets.

After a moment, he asked, "What did you mean when you said you had no expectations?"

His question startled me, enough that I answered honestly. "Just that. I didn't want you to feel pressured. You were the one, after all, who said it wasn't a great idea in the beginning. I've been known to create the impression I wanted more in the past, so I didn't want to make things weird between us."

Mack kicked a pebble as we passed from the trees into the parking lot behind the lodge. "Okay. It's not because I seem like the kind of guy who isn't worth expectations?"

Um. Okay, now I didn't know what the hell to think of that. I stopped about halfway across the parking lot and turned to look at him. "No! Why would you ask that?"

Seeing Mack anything but completely confident and comfortable in his skin was unusual. Right now, he looked like I'd never seen him before. He shifted his shoulders and rolled his head from side to side. Then he stared out toward the pasture just visible in the distance before finally bringing his gaze back to mine.

"I don't know. Just wondering."

Right then, Dawson and Walker came out the back door to the lodge, immediately veering in our direction. Dawson cast me a grin as he stopped us. "How's this little cutie doing?" he asked, rubbing his knuckles under Betty's chin.

"She's good."

Dawson held out a hand, and I passed her over. He immediately tucked her into his chest and nuzzled her.

Walker grinned. "Puppies make everyone a sap, so you better hand her to me next."

"Why don't y'all take the last two puppies? I'm sure Evie and Jade would both say yes."

Dawson's smile was wide. "I'll ask Evie tonight. We've both been so busy. You too," he said, looking toward Walker and handing the puppy over.

Mack stayed quiet. I didn't know what was up with him,

but he definitely seemed out of sorts, as if his question hadn't already made that obvious.

"Well, I need get to the clinic because I have two surgeries today. I'll see y'all later, okay?" After Walker returned Betty, I hurried off. A part of me wanted Mack to follow, but he didn't. I knew he likely had other things to do. As it was, I truly did need to get to the clinic or I'd be playing catch-up all day.

———

After a late night of playing at open mic at Lost Deer Bar, followed by hectic day at the clinic, I hurried out for a doctor's appointment I'd scheduled four months ago before I even moved home. Not because it was an emergency, but because it took that freaking long to get on the schedule for my annual appointment. I could've gone to Asheville, but I preferred the OB/GYN I'd seen when I lived here before. She was one of the few who served the valley, so she was busy. I'd been relieved to discover Jackson had kept an old car our father used to drive. Since I'd sold mine in my travels, it was handy for me to have to drive when I needed it. Like today, for example.

Dr. Hollows closed the door behind her as she stepped into the office where I was waiting. Her cheeks plumped up with her smile. "Well, hey, Ash. It's so good to see you. Have you officially moved back to Stolen Hearts Valley?"

Returning her smile, I nodded. "Yep. I knew I was coming, so I scheduled this ahead of time because I'm due for my annual."

Dr. Hollows sat on a rolling stool beside a counter. Spinning on it to face me, she tapped on a few computer keys. The paper crinkled under my legs when I swung my feet.

"Obviously, we have your history, but I haven't seen you here in this clinic for two years. Anything I should know? Any changes?"

I shook my head. "I don't think so."

She nodded and pushed her glasses up on her nose before looking back toward me. "Based on your records here, you're due for a Pap smear, so let's get started. Before I do your exam, let's get a urine sample. When I haven't seen a patient for over a year, I like to do the full battery. Should I be concerned about STD testing or anything else?"

"I don't think so, but if you think it would be smart, I'll go for it."

She gave a matter-of-fact nod. "Might as well. Bathroom's right there." She pointed at a door inside the office where we were.

A few minutes later, I had my feet in the stirrups and my knee splayed out in the usual undignified position while Dr. Hollows inserted the speculum and began her exam. We were chatting casually when she went still and lifted her head. "Are you aware your IUD fell out?

"Um, no."

Dr. Hollows nodded slowly. "The string for the IUD is gone, and I can't find any sign of it."

"Is that possible?" I squeaked.

"It's not all that common, but it *is* possible. It could've been dislodged and fallen out when you went to the bathroom or something like that. Have you been checking to make sure the string is in place?"

Staring at her, I shook my head slowly, feeling numb. "Uh, no. I haven't checked in a while." My mind spun its wheels. I was pretty sure the last time I checked was while I was still seeing Kyle. We'd used condoms every single time, so I'd gotten out of the habit of checking. For whatever reason, I hadn't thought to check since I'd been with Mack.

"I think we need to do a pregnancy test if you've been sexually active."

"Um, is that a part of the regular testing?"

She shook her head. "Only if we think it's needed.

Usually standard testing is to screen for overall health issues like diabetes."

"Okay. Well, I guess we should do that. Can you see any other signs that I'm pregnant?"

"I just started your exam, and the first thing I noticed was the missing IUD. Let's finish up."

A while later, Dr. Hollows had left the room while I changed. I was dressed and waiting in one of the chairs when she returned. She set her computer tablet on the counter before leaning her hips against it and giving me a considering look.

"Well?" I felt a little sick.

"You're pregnant."

"Are you kidding?"

"Ash, pregnancy is definitely not something I would joke about. The urine sample is positive."

"I know you said you didn't often get your period with the IUD, but do you know the last time you had your cycle?"

I shook my head. With my heartbeat thudding loudly and shock sliding through me, I couldn't really think.

"How far along do you think I am?"

"I'm going to guess about seven weeks."

Chapter Twenty-Nine

MACK

"Mack, why would you think that?" Evie asked, her brow knitted in concern.

"I know it's not rational, Evie. It's just stuck with me." My little sister narrowed her eyes and leveled me with what I supposed she thought was a glare. Evie was too cute for a glare, but I got the message. "Why are you so pissed?"

"Because you're torturing yourself over something you had absolutely no control over, and it's kind of arrogant."

"Arrogant?"

"Yes. You can't save everybody. You definitely couldn't save Krista that day. Get over it and stop letting it get in the way of your life."

"What the hell are you talking about? I'm living," I said defensively.

Evie paused to dip a tortilla chip into the bowl of salsa on the table. She'd stopped by my cabin tonight to show off the puppy she and Dawson had decided to adopt.

I waited because I didn't feel like doing anything else.

After she finished chewing, she said, "Well, as far as I can tell, you're afraid of how you feel about Ash. You haven't even said a word to me about it, and you've started avoiding her."

"What the fuck, Evie? I have not been avoiding Ash."

Evie gave me a knowing look. "You went from spending every night at her cabin to hardly at all. That's avoiding."

I closed my eyes and dropped my head. Tunneling my fingers through my hair as I sat up, I shook my head. "Wow, you've been counting?"

"Not me. Dani. If she's wrong, you wouldn't look the way you do. I have to go because I have to get to work. Think about what I said."

If I thought that was bad enough, maybe five minutes after Evie left, Ash showed up at my door. "We need to talk," she said, walking in without even offering a hello.

"About what?" I was annoyed, not with Ash, but with Evie and the frustration of everyone knowing everything around here.

Bright spots of pink crested on Ash's cheeks as she stared at me. She sucked in a breath of air and let it out in a rough sigh. "I'm pregnant."

I shook my head. I must've heard her wrong. "Huh?"

"I. Am. Pregnant." For good measure, she enunciated every word for me.

My knees actually felt weak as those words slammed into me.

"Maybe you should sit down," she suggested.

Turning, I crossed the room and slid into one of the chairs by the table. My cabin was a mirror of Ash's except I didn't have amazing coffee and lacked any homey touches. Until this week, I'd been spending almost every night with her.

I gestured to the chair across from me. "Care to join me?"

Ash was still standing with her arms wrapped around her waist by the door. After a long moment, she crossed the room silently and sat down. Her face was tense. I wasn't sure how to read the look in her eyes. Anger, concern, irritation, and more were passing through.

"How did you get pregnant? I thought you had an IUD."

Ash chewed on her bottom lip for a moment before answering, "Apparently, it fell out. I didn't know. I'm sorry."

"What are you sorry for?" I was genuinely confused.

"I'm not sure when it fell out. If you don't believe me, you can talk to my doctor."

"Ash, it's not like I would think you would lie to me about something like that."

My brain felt filled with static electricity, and I didn't know what to think. At all.

"I'll go." She stood quickly.

Panic clawed at me. I reached for her hand, catching it just as she turned away. It was ice cold. "Don't go."

Ash turned back, and I could feel tremors of tension running through her. She tugged her hand free. She looked like a wild horse about to bolt. "What do you want, Mack?"

The moment she asked that question, pieces of my own puzzle clicked into place in my mind. Ash was meant to be mine. Her pregnancy shocked the hell out of me, but it was the startling bolt of clarity I needed.

"You. I want you." My words came out slightly ragged.

Her eyes widened, and her mouth opened and closed before she shook her head. "What do you mean? I told you I didn't have any expectations. I don't want you to say you want me just because I'm pregnant."

Trepidation slid through me as I stared at her.

Chapter Thirty

ASH

You. I want you.

Mack's words drifted through my thoughts like tumble-weeds. I couldn't relax. I was trying to catch my balance, to get my feet under me, but the ground kept shifting with little earthquakes of emotion and confusion.

I hadn't expected to get pregnant. Obviously. I didn't know what I wanted for myself. However, one shining beacon of clarity was that I wanted this baby.

The timing was awful, and I had zero confidence in my relationship—if that's what I could even call it—with Mack. Maybe I hadn't been considering a baby. Hell, there was *absolutely* no maybe there. But the route of my life had carved out this new intersection, and I was going to take the path it offered.

Mack stared at me, looking worried, which almost made me laugh. Mack didn't worry much. He was all calm, cool, and collected. A baby was just as much of a surprise for him as it was for me.

"Please don't go," he said, stepping toward me and catching one of my hands with his again.

God, even just Mack holding my hand felt so good. He was a big man, tall with broad shoulders, and that face of his, it was so lived in. He was a man who carried his masculinity with no effort. With his shoulders, it wouldn't be much effort.

His big hand engulfed mine, his grip strong and easy. His thumb brushed across the back of my hand, the calloused surface sending sparks skittering over my skin and chasing up my arm to spiral through the rest of my body.

His touch was warm and comforting. I was tired and so tense, drawn tight inside. My emotions felt as if they were pressing at the surface, and I just wanted to forget everything.

As I stared into the deep pools of his blue eyes, I found I couldn't hold up all of my guard. I swallowed and nodded. "Okay."

I hadn't even changed out of my clothes from being at the vet clinic earlier. Mack dipped his head and leaned down to press a kiss on the side of my neck. "Let's get you in the shower," he murmured when he lifted his head.

"Shower?" I returned, a little confused.

"Your hands are cold." He engulfed my other hand in his, which was icy cold in contrast to his warm grip. Although the cabin was air-conditioned, I'd just come out of ninety-degree heat and should've been anything but cold.

"And you've got dirt on your cheek. Right here." He released one of my hands, and his fingertips dusted lightly over my cheek.

Minutes later, I'd left my shoes behind at the door and was climbing into the shower as Mack nudged me in. Apparently, this was a two-person job because he followed me in.

I'd gone and fallen in love with Mack, and now I was having his baby. There were so many uncertain contingencies that just trying to think about it hurt my brain. So I didn't. Think, that is.

I allowed Mack to soap my body with his hands, teasing me into a needy puddle. I let him kiss me until I forgot everything. I let him lift me and carry me out of the shower, drying me off and then burying himself inside me on the bathroom counter because we were too impatient to get to a bed.

I told him I had to go back to my place because of Betty. Mack insisted on coming with me.

You. I want you.

His words played on a loop in my brain. We fell asleep, and I savored the feel of Mack's arms holding me close as he curled around me from behind, enveloping me in his strong embrace.

Sometime in the darkness, Betty squeaked in her crate, and I woke. I reminded myself I was training her, and she needed to make it through the night. So I lay still until she quieted again. And then my mind went crazy.

Nothing was quite so maddening as the anxiety wreaking havoc in my thoughts. It felt as if my anxiety was kicking over every box in the attic of my mind and dragging out every possible scenario to worry about.

Mack said he wanted me, but that didn't mean he loved me. Kyle wanted me when it was convenient for him. Brian never loved me even though he said he did.

I was already in over my head and barely treading water in the unexpected depths of my feelings for Mack. But now, I was pregnant. And I fiercely wanted this baby. I lay awake listening to the steady rhythm of Mack's breathing and trying to calm down. Tears pricked hot in my eyes. This was definitely not a planned pregnancy, yet I wanted this baby so much it hurt.

For all I knew, I wouldn't even make it through the first trimester.

I wanted to believe in Mack. My anxiety tried to kick

some sense into my heart. *Don't be stupid about that. Don't let yourself hope for more.*

I resolved to be sensible tomorrow. It felt good, oh, so good to lose myself in the guaranteed bliss of sex with Mack. But I needed to be practical and to make a smart decision for myself and my baby. *Our* baby.

———

"I'm sorry, say that again," Shay said, her head whipping up from where she stood at the reception desk in the vet clinic.

"I'm pregnant," I repeated.

My best friend stared at me wide-eyed as her mouth fell open. The pen in her hand clattered to the floor. "Oh."

At that moment, the front door to the vet clinic opened, and the sound of crying reached my ears. Shay gave me a little glare. "We are going to discuss this further later on," she hissed.

I'd chosen this afternoon to talk to her because the clinic was empty except for us. Jackson and the rest of the first responder crew were out on an overnight training exercise. The vet tech was also out of town this week.

I wasn't thrilled with the interruption either, but I knew I would have plenty of time to talk to Shay later. Turning, I faced a woman holding an injured cat in one arm with her crying daughter trailing at her side.

I reached reflexively to the box of latex gloves tucked around the edge of the reception counter and snapped them on quickly as I approached her. "Hey there," I said, using my calmest voice. "What happened?"

The harried mother gratefully relinquished the cat into my arms. As I began inspecting him, noting it appeared he'd taken a blow to his shoulder, she explained, "He ran across the street and kind of bounced off the edge of a car's tire. Fortunately, they were going really slow, but he just laid there." She looked down at her daughter. "Honey, we're at the vet. She's going to make George all better. That's her job."

When her eyes shifted to mine, I smiled encouragingly. "I think we can do that."

I was pretty confident. The little guy looked very uncomfortable and hissed at me as I gently probed his shoulder, but he was breathing okay.

"Let me go ahead and take him right back. I'm gonna need y'all to wait here. There are toys in the corner, and some snacks right there," I said, gesturing with my head toward the wall where we had a small cart that held water, tea, juice, and snacks. "It's just Shay here with me this afternoon. She'll come back with me to get started, but she'll be back soon with an update. Okay?"

At the little girl's tearful nod and the mother's thank you, I hurried down the hall with Shay. She was quiet until we were in an evaluation room with the door firmly closed. "Is he really going to be okay?" she asked immediately.

"I think so, or I wouldn't have said anything." I set the cat on the stainless-steel table. "I'm going to need to sedate him so I can examine him more thoroughly."

In a matter of minutes, George was resting comfortably. An X-ray determined he had a fracture just below his shoulder.

"You're a lucky guy," I murmured as I carefully worked.

Shay came in to check just as I was finishing up. "How's he doing?"

"He'll be fine," I said firmly.

"Good. Just so you know, your rain check on that announcement only lasts until this is over."

I laughed softly as she left the room to give the family an update. Not much later, I was able to send George home. The little girl was beaming from ear to ear and promising me up and down she was going to take the best care of him ever.

As soon as I closed the door behind them, Shay's voice

reached me from behind. "Go ahead and lock it. It's after five."

After locking the door, I returned to the reception desk and leaned my elbows on it. "Sorry to spring that on you like that. My timing was bad."

"Ya think?" she muttered as she closed a file cabinet and locked it before turning to power down the computer. "Let's go over to the farmhouse. I have a new bottle of wine from Lost Deer Winery, and we'll have the house to ourselves. Well, except for Pepper." She was referring to their beloved dog.

"I can bring Betty, right?" I crossed the waiting room to check on the puppy who was sound asleep in the playpen in the corner.

"Of course you can. Let's get going. I need details."

Only minutes later, we had crossed the parking area from the vet clinic to the farmhouse, the very house where I grew up and where Shay and Jackson now lived. The English Setter they'd adopted from the rescue program was eating dinner.

"Okay, I can multitask," Shay called as she carried a bottle of wine over to the table. "You're pregnant?"

"I didn't mean to freak you out. Yes."

"Are you okay with this? Do you want a baby? I'll support whatever you need. If you need me to go to labor classes with you, I'm there. If you need me to hold your hand when you go get an abortion, I'm there."

"I want to have the baby," I said firmly. "I've had three days to adjust to the news."

"You waited three days to tell me this?!" She finished pouring her glass of wine and immediately took a big gulp. "Fill your own." She pointed at the wine bottle after she swallowed.

"Um, I'm not drinking wine," I offered with a wry smile.

Shay slapped her hand to her forehead. "Duh. Let me get you some water."

In another moment, she'd returned to the table and handed me a glass of water before sitting down. "I just needed time to absorb it. It's Mack's, if you were wondering."

"Well, I figured. You never were one to sleep around. Not that there would be anything wrong with it if you were," she added hastily while I laughed.

I reached for a piece of cheese from the small platter of crackers, cheese, and fruit she'd set between us while she reheated some leftover pizza from Dani at the lodge restaurant.

After a bite of cheese, I took a breath and answered. "I want to have the baby. I didn't plan it. Obviously."

Shay eyed me steadily. "I'll toast for you. Babies make me happy." She lifted her wineglass, clinking it on my water glass when I held it up.

After another breath, I added, "I told Mack."

"How did he take the news?"

"I think he was shocked, but then, so was I." I ate another piece of cheese and pondered what to say next. "I don't know what to do about Mack. He says he wants me. Before this news, I told him I didn't have any expectations. Being serious isn't exactly on his radar."

"What do you want from him?" Shay's question was voiced softly.

Emotion tightened in my chest and throat, and I took another gulp of my ice water. "I love him. I just don't know if he feels the same way."

"Have you asked him?"

I almost spit out my next sip of water. "No! Asking something like that could definitely be perceived as pressure. You know how pressure went for me before. Brian said I pressured him by getting excited about weddings. I tried not to pressure Kyle, and then I ended up just feeling like an idiot. There's no way I'm asking Mack if he loves me. I'll pass on feeling like a total idiot *yet again*."

"What are y'all doing right now?"

I shrugged. "Because I'm weak, I had sex with him the other night, but I haven't since. I think I need to keep it on friends-only turf until we figure out how we both feel."

Shay was quiet, a twitch of worry between her eyes. "I think you should tell him how you feel, but that's your call. If you don't mind me asking, were you on birth control?"

I rolled my eyes. "I'll talk to Mack when I'm ready. To your question, I had an IUD. I went for my annual, and the first thing Dr. Hollows asked me was if I knew my IUD had fallen out. I didn't know they could fall out."

Shay started laughing. "I guess they can."

"They do say no birth control is foolproof except abstinence," I said dryly. "So if you don't want to get pregnant..."

Shay's cheeks went pink. "I'm not gonna stop having sex."

"That's totally fine. Just please don't give me any details about you and my brother."

Chapter Thirty-One

MACK

Jackson eyed me warily. "I'm sorry, what?"

"I need some advice," I repeated. "But I'd appreciate it if you didn't hit me first."

Jackson leaned back in his chair. "Fuck my life. Please don't tell me you're asking for advice about you and my sister."

"Yes, I am. Because you know her, and I could seriously use some advice."

We were at a diner, Candy's Diner to be specific. Dawson had turned us onto this place because it was run by an old family friend of his. The friend in question, Candy, stopped by our table. "Hey, y'all. I'm assuming you'd like to start with coffee?"

She was already filling the mugs by our elbows before we even answered. It was six a.m., so we definitely needed coffee.

"I need it as strong as you've got," Jackson said.

"I have a new espresso maker," Candy said as she reached up and pulled out the pencil tucked behind her ear. "Do you know what else you want? I'll go ahead and get your order started."

"Give us both a test drive with that new espresso machine," I interjected. "Otherwise, I'll take one of your omelets. I don't care what kind, just make sure there's bacon in it."

"Same," Jackson replied.

"Be back with your new coffee in just a few." Candy walked off, and I took a sip of coffee.

It was quiet for a moment, and then Jackson gave me a firm look. "Well, spit it out, dude."

"I will, but I need you to promise not to mention to Ash that I talked to you about this."

Jackson sighed. "I promise."

"I'm not sure what's going on, but Ash is cutting me out, and she's pregnant."

Jackson choked on a sip of coffee. I handed over a napkin and grabbed another to wipe the coffee splatter off the table. "Sorry, bad timing."

"Ya think?" he muttered. He regarded me for a moment. "It's a good thing we're in public. Otherwise, I'd seriously consider kicking your ass."

"I get it. Ash just told me the other day, and now she's basically avoiding me. I don't know what to do, and I'm in love with her."

Saying that word out loud snatched the breath out of my chest. But I needed to say it. I'd known it, but somehow, those four letters strung together scared the hell out of me.

Candy arrived at that moment. "Here y'all go." She set our two fresh coffees down with a flourish. "I made you both an Americano with two shots of espresso. That should definitely wake you up. Your food will be out in just a few. I'll take those old coffees." She snagged the two mugs with one hand and patted me on the shoulder as she hurried off to check on the next table. This diner was small, but it was always busy.

Jackson and I took a moment to taste the new coffee. "Oh man, that's good," I said, appreciating the rich, dark flavor.

"Agreed," Jackson replied with a satisfied sigh as he set his mug down. "Now, what is it you want my advice with? The fact that you got my sister pregnant, or the fact you're in love with her?"

Strangely, I needed no advice about the surprise pregnancy. I would support whatever Ash wanted. She'd told me plainly that night she wanted our baby, so I was one hundred percent with her. Maybe I didn't plan it, maybe I didn't ever expect to have kids, but I wanted our baby with a fierceness that surprised me. Every protective instinct inside me was on fire and determined to make sure everything turned out better than okay.

"Maybe it's crazy," I began, "but even though the pregnancy surprised the hell out of me, I'll be there however Ash wants me to be. That's the rub, though. I don't know what she wants. With me."

Jackson stared at me quietly and took an almost aggressive swallow of his coffee.

"Look, I get that you're pissed—"

Jackson nodded sharply. "Yeah, I'm fucking pissed. You got my sister pregnant. What the fuck? And I can't believe you asked me not to say anything to her about this."

Candy arrived with our food. After she set our plates down, she looked back and forth between us. "What's wrong, y'all? Things look a little tense."

"Mack got my sister pregnant," Jackson said flatly.

Candy's gaze was careful. "Well, does she want the baby?" When I nodded, a smile broke out on her face. "Then congratulations! Every baby is worth celebrating." Her gaze softened as she looked toward Jackson. "Now, I'm sure you're feeling all manly and like you need to defend your sister's honor or something like that, but unless Mack is an asshole, and unless she doesn't want anything to do with him, then be pissed and move on. I'm sure your sister and Mack could use your support."

Jackson stuck his tongue in his cheek as he let out a sharp laugh. "Right. I get it. I wasn't even used to them being together, and now she's pregnant. And apparently, he's in love with her, and she's ignoring him. He wanted my advice. I think you have better advice to offer than I do, Candy."

Candy squeezed his shoulder. "You're a good friend and a good older brother." Her attention came back to me. "If you love her, you gotta show her. I don't know what's going on because I've never met Jackson's sister. What's her name?"

"Ashley. She goes by Ash."

"I'm sure Ash is lovely because she's Jackson's sister and you love her." Jackson let out a heavy sigh, but Candy ignored him. "Just tell her what you feel. You have to communicate with your words and your actions. You have to be there. Not just for the easy stuff either. If you don't mind me being blunt, if the sex is good, then that qualifies as easy. Now you get your butt back to Stolen Hearts and set the record straight with her. I don't know if she's in love with you, but there's only one way for you to find out. If she's not, suck it up and be a good father and a good partner to her in taking care of your child."

On the heels of that little lecture, Candy gave my shoulder an enthusiastic squeeze and hurried off because her husband was calling her name from the kitchen.

"What she said," Jackson added, gesturing with his fork in the direction of the kitchen.

"Do you still feel like hitting me?" I asked after we ate in silence for a few minutes. The food was delicious and a good enough distraction that I'd calmed down a little bit.

Jackson finished chewing and took a swallow of water before replying, "I'm not sure yet. Depends on how Ash is doing. That also depends on you letting her know you told me what the fuck is going on."

Chapter Thirty-Two

ASH

Being overly nervous now that I knew I wanted my baby, I had scheduled an appointment with Dr. Hollows. In my hand, I had a list of questions I'd scribbled on a piece of paper.

Her medical assistant had just told me that she was running late today after an emergency surgery, so it was going to be a few minutes. I sat in the chair beside the examination table, the little piece of paper warm and slightly crumpled in my fingers. I unfolded it, smoothing it on my thigh as I scanned the questions again. There was a light knock on the door, and I called for whomever it was to come in.

The med assistant poked her head around the door. "Your boyfriend's here," she said, her eyes twinkling.

I silently groaned. *How the hell did Mack figure out I was here?* I didn't want to make a scene and make it any more awkward than necessary, so I pasted a smile on my face. "Okay, send him on back."

She disappeared, and I heard her voice saying, "Go on in. She's waiting for the doctor. It's going to be a few minutes."

Mack's tall form filled the doorway as he stepped through. The sound of the door closing behind him clicked loudly in the quiet exam room. My heart felt lodged in my throat.

I'd totally been avoiding him. It had now been three days since we talked. After my talk with Shay while he was gone for the night with the rest of the crew, the following day I'd been crazy busy in the clinic. Jackson and the rest of the crew hadn't even been scheduled to return until then. By the time I finished an emergency surgery on a dog who'd been hit on the highway, it was close to midnight. Jackson had offered to take duty at the clinic and sleep on the small bed we kept in one of the rooms there, but I needed to be there. I just couldn't leave for the night. I knew I wasn't going to feel okay if the dog didn't make it. Thank God she did.

I was running on fumes and no coffee. My emotions were on the raw side. Mack stood by the door for a moment. He was such a big guy, and his presence filled the space.

Biting back a sigh, I gestured him closer. "You might as well sit down."

In three strides, he was sliding his hips into the chair beside me, his big blue eyes searching my face. He looked as tired as I felt, and my heart gave a kick. He curled his big palm over mine where it rested on my thigh. His touch was always warm and comfortable, a port in the storm of my messy life. My emotions felt akin to whirling dervish.

"Are you okay?" he asked, a crease of worry between his brows.

I couldn't seem to speak, so I tried valiantly to breathe through the tightness in my chest. I *so* did not want to cry right now, but tears were wicking up from the knot in my throat and pressing hot at the backs of my eyes.

I needed to say something, but I could only manage to nod.

"I love you," he said, so solemnly that all I could do was believe him.

My heart felt like it was going to crack open inside my chest. Joy burst through all of my emotional confusion.

"Is that okay?"

"Is it okay if you love me?" I finally managed to ask, my voice coming out raspy.

"Well, yeah," Mack said, uncertainty dashing through his eyes. "You've been avoiding me for days. I've never been in love, so I really have no idea how to do this. I thought maybe I needed to tell you how I felt, and then we could go from there."

Before I could formulate a response, he added, "Don't get pissed off at Shay, but she's the one who told me you had this appointment. I thought maybe you should know I want to be here for any appointments for you and for the baby."

Well, that did it. I burst into noisy tears. Mack looked flabbergasted and frightened by my display. His hand slid up my back and rubbed in circles. "I didn't mean to make you cry," he muttered.

Then he was pulling me onto his lap, which was awkward because the chairs weren't very big. Considering his size in relation to mine, sitting on Mack's lap had me feeling like a girl. I tucked my head into the crook of his neck and breathed him in. His warmth and strength and comfort helped ease the emotions rioting inside me. I reached the hiccupping stage in my tears. I felt him shift, and then he was handing me a tissue he must've found on the counter beside him.

I blew my nose and finally lifted my head. "I didn't mean to cry."

"S'okay. I just want you to be okay, Ash. If you don't love me, that's okay too. We'll deal with it."

Oh, geez. Now he had me crying again. Mack being sweet was dangerous for my emotional sanity.

"I do love you," I said between sniffles and a few hiccups.

Mack leaned his head back, whispering roughly, "Oh, thank Jesus."

When he lowered his head, there was a knock on the door. I moved to scramble out of Mack's lap, but he held me tight. "You're not going anywhere. I finally got you back in my arms. I need a few minutes."

I started laughing, and the door opened. Dr. Hollows peered into the room. "Oops, looks like I'm interrupting a moment. If you don't mind, I'll check on the next patient and come back. Sound good?"

"Perfect," I replied.

I blew my nose after she closed the door.

I looked up at Mack, feeling sheepish. "I've been avoiding you."

"Really?" he drawled. "I hadn't noticed."

I took a shuddery breath. "I'm sorry. This pregnancy was a surprise and kind of threw me. I was afraid you didn't love me, and I didn't want to pressure you. I've done that before, even if I didn't mean to, and it didn't turn out so well."

He searched my eyes, lifting a hand and swiping a tear away with his thumb. "It's okay. I've been avoiding in my own way. It took me a while to figure out I loved you. Don't you dare think it's because we're having a baby. I just needed some time to catch up. And get a lecture from Evie and Candy."

"Candy?" I queried, completely confused.

"Oh, Candy's Diner in Asheville. Candy runs it. She's an old family friend of Dawson's. He started taking us there when we go to Asheville. She's been married for over fifty years, so I took her advice."

I laughed, leaning up to press a kiss on the side of his neck. When I drew away, he looked worried. "What is it?"

"You're probably going to kick my ass, but I told Jackson. Because I needed advice. Desperately."

Chapter Thirty-Three

MACK

Ash's eyes widened. Her mouth parted before she closed it again and angled her head to the side. A tear fell from her eyelashes, and I brushed it away with my thumb.

"I'll understand if you're pissed about me talking to Jackson," I added.

My heart was thundering along in my chest, although the tightness I'd been holding there for days started to loosen, and the cold dread balled in my stomach was dissolving.

"I'm not thrilled, but I understand. I think."

I rushed to explain. "You were avoiding me completely, so we didn't have a chance to talk, and I didn't know what to do. Jackson's seriously pissed off with me."

"I'll talk to him," Ash offered.

"You don't need to talk to him on my behalf. You're his little sister, and I got you pregnant."

Ash bit her lip, and then a laugh slipped out. I was almost giddy with relief.

"It'll be fine. Jackson will get over it. After all, Remy was as close to him as you were when y'all were growing up. Jackson's with Shay," she explained, referencing Shay's older brother who had moved to Alaska a while back.

I shrugged. "I'm not gonna argue the point with Jackson. He can be mad. All that matters, is us."

Ash traced a finger along my collarbone before leaning forward to drop a kiss in the divot at the base of my throat. Cupping her cheek, I nudged her chin up and dusted my lips over hers. I meant for it to be a brief kiss. I was, surprisingly, aware of where we were, after all.

Ash arched into me, sliding her hand around the base of my neck and pulling me closer. Her tongue slipped out to tease mine. Before I knew it, she was straddling me and rocking her hips over my arousal.

Fuck me. Ash made me forget where we were until I heard footsteps in the hallway. I pulled my lips free from hers, my head thumping the wall.

"Fuck, Ash," I groaned. "Let me keep my shit together."

"Maybe I don't want you to," she teased with another shimmy of her hips.

I narrowed my eyes and lifted her firmly off my lap. She wiggled but laughed.

Only seconds later, the doctor knocked on the door again. Ash called, "Come in!"

The doctor stepped through the doorway. Ash gestured between us. "This is Dr. Hollows. This is Mack, my boyfriend."

It was such a small thing, really, but my heart swelled at hearing her call me that. Ash didn't know it yet, but we weren't just going to be boyfriend and girlfriend. She was mine, and I intended to make it official.

Dr. Hollows smiled at us. "Is it presumptuous for me to guess you're the father?"

"He is," Ash said firmly as I nodded.

The doctor smiled. "I'm glad you're here. It's important for you to be a part of this with Ash. It's a team effort. I am all about women doing things independently, but when they have someone who's willing to do it with them, I'm your biggest cheerleader." She narrowed her eyes in my direction as she slipped her hips onto a stool across from us. "Unless, that is, you do anything to make me question whether you're a good support for Ash and your baby."

I inclined my head. "Understood."

"Now, Ash, I understand you have some questions. You certainly don't need to come in this soon, but I thought it best that we go ahead and meet so we can put your mind at ease."

Ash leaned down to pick up the piece of paper that had fallen earlier. She unfolded it and smoothed it out before handing it to the doctor.

"Oh, wow," the doctor said, a smile teasing at the corners of her mouth. "This is quite the list of questions. Let's go through them one by one. This will be helpful for both of you."

She quickly ran through Ash's questions. I didn't like learning Ash was feeling so tired some days, but relieved that was apparently normal. The doctor advised Ash to expect morning sickness soon but said she might get lucky and avoid it altogether since she was already in the timeframe when it usually started.

"And now, to your last question. Is it safe to have sex?" She smiled at us. "Absolutely. If at any point that changes, I'll let you know. Since the beginning of humanity, women have been having sex through pregnancies and delivering perfectly healthy babies. Occasionally, some complications can arise, but we'll cross that bridge if and when it comes. You're healthy, and there's no indication you need to worry at this stage."

By the time we left, I was a little shell-shocked. The enormity of Ash's pregnancy and what it was going to mean for her, for us, and for our families was crashing over me in waves. There were so many logistics to consider.

We stopped beside Ash's car, and I looked down at her.

"Can you ride back to the lodge with me? I'm not ready to leave your side."

Ash let out a surprised laugh. "I need my car."

"I'll come back and get it later. I promise. I'll have one of the guys bring me out to pick it up."

With a bemused smile, she shrugged. "Okay."

Moments later, I was driving back to the lodge. "We need a house."

When I slid my eyes sideways to glance at Ash, her mouth was open, and she was staring at me like I was crazy.

"Wha-at?"

"We need a house," I repeated. "I mean, we could make it work in one of the cabins, but that's pretty tight. I can build our house. Let's talk to Jackson about options."

Ash sputtered. "Now we're building a house. I can't believe this."

"I'm pretty sure having a baby is more monumental than building a house," I offered.

Ash started laughing so hard that she was wiping tears away from her eyes, and I was concerned.

"Are you okay? I didn't mean to make you cry. Again."

She shook her head as she swiped at her tears. "Those aren't sad tears. It's all, um, a bit much. How did we get from neither of us not wanting any expectations to having a baby and building a house?"

I reached over the console between the seats and caught her hand, giving it a squeeze. I didn't let go because I needed to touch her. "I don't know about you, but I just needed enough time and sense to figure it out. That's all. You're mine, Ash girl. And we're having a baby, and it's all good."

She smiled over at me as I slowed to exit off the highway. "Do you think we can do this?"

"I *know* we can do this."

My heart gave a rounding kick in emphasis. I felt filled to the brim with feeling, all of it good.

After we got back to the lodge, I was holding Ash's hand

as we walked across the parking lot toward the staff kitchen. I stopped and gave her hand a little tug. She turned immediately, her brows lifting in question.

"Mind letting Jackson know we talked? Then I can go ahead and get it over with."

"Get what over with?"

"In case he wants to hit me. I'd rather deal with it today."

Ash's eyes went wide, and she shook her head wildly. "He doesn't get to hit you. I went into this with my eyes wide open."

I shrugged. "We'll see."

Whether or not he knew we were talking about him, at that moment, Jackson came striding through the trees on the opposite side of the parking lot. When he saw us, his stride slowed briefly before he picked it up again and crossed to stand in front of us. "Well?"

Ash tightened her fingers where they were laced with mine and lifted her chin. "Mack told me y'all talked. We're fine. In fact, we're great. You do *not* need to be all overprotective and threaten to kick his ass. Or worse yet, to actually kick his ass."

Jackson's alert gaze bounced from Ash to me. "Glad to hear it. For what it's worth, just because you don't want me to be pissed off at Mack doesn't mean I won't be."

Ash let out an annoyed sigh and rolled her eyes. "You are such a man."

I almost laughed because Ash had recently made that comment to me.

"Is that supposed to be an insult?" Jackson countered. "Because, in case you missed it, I *am* a man."

Ash huffed again. "Whatever."

She moved to begin walking again when Jackson asked, "Mind if I have a minute with Mack?"

Ash's hair rippled over her shoulders as she turned back. "As long as you're not gonna be an asshole."

Jackson gave her a long look, but he remained silent.

I squeezed her hand. "Babe, it's fine. I'll see you in a few."

As soon as the door to the staff kitchen closed, Jackson hooked a thumb in one of his pockets. "I'm not going to kick your ass. Not here."

I shrugged. "If it'll make you feel better, go right ahead," I offered.

Jackson chuckled. "As long as Ash is happy, I'm good. If you hurt her"—his voice went low—"we'll revisit this."

"I won't hurt her. I love her."

Jackson studied me before nodding firmly. "I believe you. But love is never easy."

After a beat, he closed the distance between us and clapped me on the shoulder in something of a half hug. "Now, go tell Ash I didn't kick your ass."

When I walked into the kitchen a moment later, I looked across the room to see Ash standing by the windows, looking out at the mountains. The sun was dropping in the sky. The blue haze above the mountains was shot through with silvery-gold light and shades of pink and lavender.

It was beautiful, but my focus was on Ash. Her brown hair fell in tousled waves over her shoulders. She wore jeans and a T-shirt, nothing remarkable. Yet she was so gorgeous —to me—that my breath seized in my lungs for a moment. On a rushing exhale, my heart kicked up a racket inside my chest.

Although I distantly heard the hum of voices around me, my entire lens narrowed to Ash as I crossed the room to her. When I slipped my arms around her waist from behind, she jumped a little. A smile curved on her cheek when she angled her head back and saw me.

"Oh, it's you," she said softly.

"Who else would it be?"

Biting her lip, she shrugged. "No one." She spun in my arms, her eyes coasting over my face. "I don't see any bruises."

I chuckled. "Nah. Jackson didn't hit me. If I don't keep you happy, though, he might."

Ash dipped her head and pressed her lips to the corner of my collarbone. "No worries on that account."

My skin felt lit by a flame at that tiny spot with heat zinging through me. Sliding a hand to cup her nape, I bent low to kiss her. Just a quick kiss. But then, Ash's tongue snuck out to play with mine. I almost forgot where we were until a voice intruded. "Seriously? Y'all need to take this outside."

Lifting my head, I glanced sideways to find Dawson with a sly grin standing by the coffeemaker a few feet away.

"No way," Ash said firmly. "I'm starving, and I'm not missing dinner."

With her hand held in mine, we had dinner together with our friends without trying to play it cool for once. It was the best feeling ever. Ash was mine, I was hers, and I wanted the whole world to know it.

EPILOGUE
Ash

Over a year later

I splashed cold water on my face and blotted it with a towel. As I lowered it, I caught sight of myself in the mirror. My ponytail was falling down on one side, and I hadn't noticed the blob of oatmeal on my shoulder before.

Laughing softly, I shrugged. Babies were messy. Reaching into the shower for a washcloth, I wiped the oatmeal off my shoulder and then tossed it in the hamper. There was no sense in changing my shirt. Not yet. Apparently, I'd been walking around with oatmeal as a part of my outfit for most of the day.

Walking out of the bathroom, I began, "I have a new fashion statement. Oatmeal is the thing..." My words slowed and quieted when I caught sight of Mack and our baby girl.

Mack was sacked out on the couch with Molly cradled in the crook of his elbow. Her pacifier had fallen out and was resting on his chest. My breath caught for a minute, and emotion hit me in a rush.

Tired though I was—and I was more tired than I had *ever* been lately—I savored the way joy would crash through me periodically every day.

Don't get me wrong. I was never going to be a mother who glorified what it was like to have a baby who only let me sleep every night for roughly two hours at a time. I wasn't counting the hours of lost sleep because that would be too depressing. I was pretty sure the longest uninterrupted chunk of sleep I'd had was three hours in the almost year that had passed since Molly came into our world. I'd become the queen of catnaps.

But *this*—seeing the man I loved with all of my heart holding our little girl who also occupied every corner of my heart—was the best thing ever. There were lots of best things ever lately.

Those splashes of light and joy made up for being tired, and sometimes frustrated, and most of the time feeling like I was stumbling through every minute of every day. Not for the first time did I wish there was an official instruction manual for being a mother.

Tiptoeing across the room, I lifted the pacifier off Mack's chest silently, resisting the urge to press a kiss to his cheek and Molly's. No one needed to wake up. Sleep was more precious than gold these days.

Mack had built the house we were living in now. We were only a mile or so down the road from the farmhouse where I'd grown up. Seeing as Jackson and I had jointly inherited the farm, there was more than enough land to choose from. We'd picked a spot near a small pond with a pretty view of the valley.

I stole time for a shower while Mack and Molly were sleeping and changed my shirt after all. A little later, Mack came walking in the kitchen with Molly wiggling in his arms. She had Mack's eyes and his hair. While we both had brown hair, his was a shade darker than mine.

The moment Molly saw me, she let out a squeal and

bounced up and down on his arm. Crossing the kitchen, he handed her over, leaning down to plant one of his dangerous kisses on me.

When he pulled away, I was a little breathless. "You can't do that," I whispered.

"Why not?"

"Because you get me hot and bothered, and we can't do anything about it," I protested.

I was instantly distracted when Molly curled her fist around my hair, which was down at the moment. She made a gurgling sound, and I turned my attention to her. "Hey, sweetie. Did you have a nice nap with Daddy?"

"Smells good," Mack commented as Molly gurgled her reply to me. "What's in the oven?"

"Lasagna. I thought we needed something filling," I explained.

Without me needing to ask, Mack fetched a prepared bottle from the refrigerator and heated it in the microwave. We were slowly weaning Molly from nursing. Every bottle contained my breast milk, although I couldn't wait to stop pumping. Aside from lack of sleep, pumping breast milk was my least favorite part of being a mother.

Mack was the best kind of dad and partner. I never had to ask for much of anything for help. Take now, for instance. As soon as the bottle was heated, he lifted Molly from my arms and sat down at the kitchen table to feed her.

After Molly guzzled her bottle of breast milk, she conked out again. She'd spent the morning at the vet clinic being oohed and aahed over and was conveniently exhausted. When Mack returned to the kitchen after putting her in her crib, I was starting an evening pot of coffee.

He came up behind me, curling his hands on either side of the counter by my hips and dropping his head into the curve of my neck. A full-body shiver raced through me when he dusted kisses lightly behind my ear and along my neck.

"Mmm. You smell good," he murmured.

"Definitely better than dried oatmeal," I returned with a small laugh as I spun to face him in the cage of his arms.

One of his brows hitched up in question. "While you were napping, I discovered I'd been walking around all day with oatmeal on my shoulder. She had oatmeal for breakfast, so... Maybe we should get into oatmeal more."

"Like a fetish?" The slow stretch of a smile across his face sent my belly into a spin, and butterflies twirled inside.

I giggled and leaned up to press a kiss on his jaw. "She's asleep."

"I know. I was thinking we could really go crazy," he said, wagging his eyebrows suggestively.

"Oh, yeah?"

"Yeah. Let's take a nap."

Reaching behind me, I turned off the coffee I'd just started. "Lead the way," I said, dead serious.

Minutes later, still fully clothed, I fell asleep with Mack's arms hugging me close to his side. We were too tired to even undress and get under the covers.

It was pure bliss.

MACK

A few months later or so

"Dude, you've got to see this." I scrolled through my phone to the video I wanted and hit play before handing it across the table.

Dawson reached for it. He dutifully nodded and then looked up. "Molly is walking like a champ. That's cool. Hasn't she been walking for a few months now?"

"That's not just cool; it's amazing. She's a master," I protested.

Jackson, who was entering from the back door where the offices were, started laughing as he heard my comment. "Everything Molly does is amazing, according to Mack."

"Well, it is."

Dawson flashed a grin as he leaned forward to snag a cookie from the tray in the center of the table. "Just think, it wasn't that long ago that you didn't even know what to do with her."

I rolled my eyes. "I figured it out."

Jackson slid onto the bench at the other end. "Like you were a pro at first," he teased Dawson.

By chance, Evie had gotten pregnant only a few months after Ash, so Dawson followed me into fatherhood. Shay had a baby right around the same time too, which meant Jackson was right there with us on the learning curve of parenting. It still amazed me that I'd become a father first among our friends.

A little while later, I had Molly on my lap and Ash sitting beside me. As I looked around the table filled with our friends and family, I marveled that I'd ever wanted to stay away from Stolen Hearts Valley. Despite my winding path home, I was relieved I'd finally faced the ghosts that had chased me away. I would always miss my sister, but I could still have all the blessings that I denied myself for a few years.

Ash and Molly were so much of my life now that it was hard to ever imagine I'd lived without them.

Later that night, after I read Molly her bedtime story and she was down for the count, I closed the door quietly behind her and made a beeline for the bathroom.

For the past month, Molly had finally begun sleeping through the night. It was freaking awesome. I'd heard the shower start and knew Ash was in there. I needed a shower. Actually, what I needed was Ash. Shucking off my clothes, I tossed them in the hamper and stepped into the steam-filled shower.

Bubbles were sliding over Ash's curves, and her skin was rosy pink from the hot water. Stepping behind her, I slid my hands down her sides as the water rained over us.

"Can I borrow the soap?" I murmured right before I nipped at the back of her neck. My arousal was hard and insistent and conveniently resting in the slippery cleft of her bottom.

Ash giggled before handing it over her shoulder. "Oh, I didn't mean that soap. I meant the soap on you."

I slid my hands around her belly, bringing one up to tease her breasts while the other dipped down between her thighs to find her hot, slick, and ready. Just for me.

When I heard her soft moan as I slid one finger and then another inside her, I spun her around quickly. "I don't think I can wait."

"Please don't," Ash gasped when she reached between us, giving me a firm stroke with her palm.

Lifting her against me and using the wall for an assist, I sank home inside her. That was what Ash was to me—home.

Pleasure with Ash was always too much and never enough. My release crashed through me before I could savor her as much as I wanted. But then, I needed a lifetime to wring every drop out of what we had together.

After we dried off and were lounging in bed, Ash walked her fingers across my chest. The light from a lamp by the bed caught on her wedding band.

All that time I never thought I'd get serious with anyone. The minute I fell, I was *all* in. I asked Ash to marry me only weeks after she told me she was pregnant. I had to be patient because she had more baggage than me around the idea of a wedding. But it had happened, and here we were.

"Sooooo," she began, "what do you think?"

"About what?"

"It's been over a year, and we made it through the worst of Molly not sleeping. Are you bored yet?"

I lifted a hand to brush a wayward lock of hair off her cheek. "Babe, I'd happily be bored with you forever."

Ash's giggle spun around my heart, and we fell asleep.

———

Thank you for reading Steal My Heart - I hope you loved Ash & Mack's story!

Want more small town romance with alpha heroes & smart, sassy heroines? Crash Into You kicks off the Dare With Me Series.

The first time Flynn meets Daphne, she ends up covered in mud. Flynn thinks this princess needs to find the first plane out of Alaska, but Daphne needs a fresh start like nobody's business, and she's not going anywhere.

Flynn is a hot, broody, rescue-y kind of guy. He's so alpha, Daphne wants nothing more than to take him down a notch. She does manage to bring him to his knees, although she didn't expect it to make her melt at the same time.

Flynn & Daphne's story is emotional, powerful & hot enough to singe the pages.

Keep reading for a sneak peek!

Be sure to sign up for my newsletter for the latest news, teasers & more! Click here to sign up: http://jhcroixauthor.com/subscribe/

EXCERPT: CRASH INTO YOU

Daphne

A moose lumbered across the road in front of me, and I came to an abrupt stop, the SUV jerking when I slammed my foot on the brakes. "Holy shit!"

No one was in the SUV with me to hear my irreverent reaction. Although I'd done some research and knew wildlife was abundant in Alaska, it was still rather startling.

While the moose appeared to be moving slowly, its long stride covered the ground at a deceptively quick pace. Inside of a few seconds, the animal had crossed the road into a field abloom in fuchsia flowers. Its rump disappeared into a cluster of evergreen trees. I gave my head a small shake and realized I was stopped in the middle of a highway. It wasn't exactly busy, but nonetheless, it *was* a highway.

Laughing to myself, I eased off the brake and put my foot on the gas pedal again. Alaska's roads weren't crowded. As I glanced to the side while picking up speed, my breath caught at the ocean glinting under the sunshine splashing across its surface.

To one side of this highway was mountains and trees, and to the other was Cook Inlet, stretching inland from the

Pacific Ocean into Alaska. I'd already counted two glaciers and marveled at the way the ocean lapped at the base of the mountains on the other side as I drove along.

My GPS wasn't being too helpful. And I'd quickly discovered that the cell reception wasn't great here either. It was spotty at best and seemed only decent when I passed through the small towns scattered along this highway, which could take me to the farthest western point in the United States if I followed it that far.

"Dammit," I said as I glanced at the GPS on my dashboard screen.

The marker on the map still showed me sitting in a parking lot in Anchorage. "Please don't tell me you're broken."

I wished the friendly computerized voice would assure me she was not, in fact, broken. But she—the GPS voice in this SUV I'd rented, that is—remained stubbornly silent at my plea.

"Thanks for nothing," I muttered.

Anxiety, the worst kind of close friend, tightened in my chest. For the past year and a half of my life, I felt as if I'd been flung off a cliff with nothing in sight. I still felt as if I was spinning helplessly, trying to find a sense of equilibrium and somewhere to land. The last thing I needed was to get geographically lost rather than being metaphorically lost in my mind and heart.

"It's okay," I assured myself. "You know where you're going."

Side note: emotional trauma could lead to lots of soliloquies. Out loud. Thank God, I was alone more often than not, or I was certain people might consider me crazy.

Roughly an hour later, I was cursing my silly decision to try to be easy-going about my planning. Cell reception was total shit. My GPS seemed to truly be useless. To add to the mess, my SUV apparently had some kind of electrical malfunction because the speedometer kept blinking in and out. I presumed said electrical problem was the reason my GPS had abandoned me in my time of need.

"You're just looking for the name of the resort. You can find it. There will be a sign."

Yup, conversations with myself were the thing these days.

In most places, highways had signs—lots of signs—but Alaska kept it simple. There were mileage signs marking the distance to various towns, but I hadn't seen a single billboard. I recalled reading that Alaska had banned billboards upon its inception as a state. I supposed that was nice in theory, although I really, *really* wouldn't have minded one announcing my upcoming destination right about now.

The view was spectacular, and I'd seen several more moose as I'd traveled south. The one small problem, though, was that I was flying blind. The sun was starting its bow, and I was praying to reach my destination before it disappeared behind the mountains. Although it was August, the mountain peaks still had snow. Climate change was coming, but Alaska was hanging in there, at least at some elevations.

Walker Adventures was roughly twenty miles outside of one of Alaska's gems, Diamond Creek. Diamond Creek, the adjacent town near the resort, was where I intended to spend a month. That's right, an entire month in the wilderness. Me, Daphne Bell, doing something so wildly out of the ordinary that basically everyone I knew thought I was crazy.

I needed this almost as much as I needed air. My actual life, the one I left behind, was an epic mess and littered with regret, recrimination, and almost unbearable pain. Maybe, just maybe, I could piece myself together if I was far enough away.

"Oh! A sign! All you have to say is *resort*," I muttered to the green highway sign in question. "A little specificity never hurt anyone."

Fuck it. I took that left turn. The pavement stretched for a few miles and then transitioned. "Oh, hell," I murmured as the little blue SUV rumbled confidently over the gravel road. At least I made sure to rent a trusty vehicle with 4-wheel drive.

I kept on going, telling myself the same thing over and over again. *You'll find it, you're meant to be here, and it's all going to be okay.*

Considering I was thoroughly acquainted with just how *not* okay life could be, my faith in the universe was shaky at best.

Roughly forty-five minutes later, with one wheel mired deep in a mud puddle, I was staring at a bear. "Are you a brown bear or a grizzly bear?" I asked from the safety of my SUV as said bear ambled along the opposite side of the road, giving me nothing more than a cursory glance.

"Since when do roads not have shoulders?" I looked at my cell phone and glared at the no signal warning. "Fuck you."

The bear in question had caused me to swerve off the edge of the road, promptly dropping one rear wheel deep in the mud. I tapped my GPS button on the dashboard screen but got nothing. I didn't even know if I'd been speeding on the gravel road. My SUV seemed to be working, but the bells and whistles definitely weren't.

I heard a plane above and looked up at the sky through my windshield. Mind you, I didn't dare open my window in case the bear came over and ate my face.

"Oh, the plane's landing!"

The small plane descended in the sky and appeared to be landing not too awfully far away. But as the crow flew, or in this case literally as the plane flew, it could be as far as a few miles away. I didn't dare climb out and walk. Because: bears and God only knew what else.

My stomach growled, and I slapped my hand over it. I hadn't brought enough snacks. The resort promised a dinner tonight, and I thought for sure I would get there with hours to spare, so I'd eaten my last granola bar a few hours ago.

Leaning my head back against the seat, I took a deep breath and willed myself not to cry. I was going to be fine. If I had to walk, I would walk.

I heard a rustling sound, lifted my head, and screamed.

The bear was now right outside my car! Eating blueberries. I might not be a wildlife expert, but I knew blueberries when I saw them, and I'd run my car off the side of the road beside a small patch of them.

The bear lifted his head and eyed me dispassionately. I thought the bear was a he, although I had no idea why. While I was truly scared of the bear, he was a magnificent creature with gilded brown fur. He stared at me curiously for a moment after my scream, then he lowered his head and continued to eat. Somehow, it seemed ridiculous that this giant creature was nibbling—yes, nibbling—on blueberries.

I watched quietly, forgetting my predicament and forgetting the other disaster of my life as this massive bear that could probably kill me with nothing more than a gentle swat of its paw, meandered along eating blueberries. A few moments later, the bear disappeared into the trees, and I was alone again. A shaft of loneliness struck me so hard that it took my breath away.

"Daphne, you need a plan," I told myself sternly once I managed to take a breath.

I didn't know where to even begin with a plan, except hiking down this road and hoping it took me to the resort.

That spinning anxiety, a fucking whirling dervish, picked up in my chest again. I really didn't know what to do other than walk, and I could only pray I didn't have to walk too far.

Just when I was about to lose the battle with my tears, a truck appeared around the corner of the road ahead.

"Yay!" I literally lifted my fist in a cheer. I had no idea who this was, but I prayed they would stop.

Not thinking, I clambered out of the SUV and ran to the middle of the road, waving my arms like a crazy woman.

The black truck rolled to a stop. When I saw the man behind the steering wheel, I got a little intimidated. Friendly wasn't exactly the word that came to mind at his appearance.

The truck door opened, and he stepped out. My knees suddenly felt like liquid. Oh. My. God. His eyes flicked to my SUV, where it sat hanging off the side of the road with one wheel buried in the mud before his gaze landed on me. Good thing I had a few seconds to prepare myself.

When his glacial blue eyes locked with mine, an electric jolt sizzled through my body, setting every nerve ending alight with sparks. The man was tall and just plain built. His broad shoulders filled out his T-shirt. My eyes traveled down his arms, lean and muscled with a dusting of gold hair. He wore battered and faded jeans, which dipped at the waist when he hooked his thumb in a belt loop.

My eyes didn't miss the strip of tanned skin just below his T-shirt when he tugged down the waistband and revealed one side of a muscled V. I swallowed and dragged my eyes up. He had a jaw cut from granite and starkly angled cheekbones with an aristocratic nose. His lips were perfect. And then, as if to torture me, he had a dimple in the center of his chin.

I had clearly lost my mind because I felt my cheeks heat as my skin prickled all over.

"You must be Daphne," he said, his tone crisp.

All that came out of me in return was a gurgle. This man not only stole my breath but he also snatched away my ability to speak. This was new for me.

Coming October 2020!
Crash Into You

If you love hot, small town romance, take a visit to Willow Brook, Alaska in my Into The Fire Series. Check out Burn For Me - a second chance romance for the ages. It's FREE on all retailers! Don't miss Cade & Amelia's story!

Go here to sign up for information on new releases: http://jhcroixauthor.com/subscribe/

FIND MY BOOKS

Thank you for reading Steal My Heart! I hope you enjoyed the story. If so, you can help other readers find my books in a variety of ways.

1) Write a review!
2) Sign up for my newsletter, so you can receive information about upcoming new releases & receive a FREE copy of one of my books: http://jhcroixauthor.com/subscribe/
3) Like and follow my Amazon Author page at https://amazon.com/author/jhcroix
4) Follow me on Bookbub at https://www.bookbub.com/authors/j-h-croix
5) Follow me on Instagram at https://www.instagram.com/jhcroix/
6) Like my Facebook page at https://www.facebook.com/jhcroix

———

Swoon Series
This Crazy Love
Wait For Me
Break My Fall
Truly Madly Mine
Still Go Crazy
If We Dare
Steal My Heart
Into The Fire Series
Burn For Me
Slow Burn
Burn So Bad
Hot Mess
Burn So Good
Sweet Fire
Play With Fire
Melt With You
Burn For You
Crash & Burn
Brit Boys Sports Romance
The Play
Big Win
Out Of Bounds
Play Me
Naughty Wish
Diamond Creek Alaska Novels
When Love Comes
Follow Love
Love Unbroken
Love Untamed
Tumble Into Love
Christmas Nights
Last Frontier Lodge Novels
Take Me Home
Love at Last
Just This Once

ACKNOWLEDGMENTS

So many thanks to my readers - for reading my stories, letting me know you love them, and for being awesome.

Much gratitude to Najla Qamber who created the stunning covers for this series. To my beta readers and my editor for their feedback on every story. To Terri D. for minding the details.

To my early readers - Janine, Beth P., Terri E., Heather H., Carolyne B., Kathy C. & Lynne E.

DBC is there for every book, and he still makes me laugh. My dogs keep me company for every book I write.

xoxo
J.H. Croix

www.ingramcontent.com/pod-product-compliance
Lightning Source LLC
Chambersburg PA
CBHW070930190726
48292CB00004B/1183